The Wrath of Grapes

A Complete HANGOVER Cookbook & Guide to the Art of Creative SUFFERING

Patrick Meanor

XOXOX

Table of Contents

The **WRATH** OF *Grapes*

*This book is dedicated
to writer, director and actor
Edward Burns—my most
remarkable writing student.
Now, teaching me.*

P R E S S

GAMBIER, OHIO

see us at WWW.XOXOXPRESS.COM
write us at XOXOXPRESS@YAHOO.COM

Annotated Table of Contents

CHAPTER ONE: THE WRATH OF GRAPES—MORNING DREAD AND WHAT *NOT* TO DO

This chapter issues various warnings for avoiding behaviors that could increase your discomfort. AVOID at all costs consuming ANY alcoholic beverage, simply because that act is NOT a remedy for your hangover: IT'S A CONTINUATION OF THE DRUNK. And a massive failure of the imagination, your *only* ally on mornings after. We note recurring dangers to the hungover sensibility such as "Hangover Guilt," embarrassing "Hangover Malapropisms," the "Dracula Sunlight Syndrome," and "Dog's Eyes Syndrome" along with listings of the kinds of TV shows, music, media and spectacle to avoid. For example, under no circumstances should you watch documentaries on spiders, monkeys or the desperate lives of wildebeests (also known as the gnu).

CHAPTER TWO: MORE WRATH—WHAT *TO* DO

This chapter explains the need for a comprehensive hangover treatment and properly defines the word by tracing its history in a number of foreign languages. The chapter also discusses the physical and metaphysical factors that determine the severity of the hangover and surveys a variety of symptoms that must be treated. It proposes as specific treatment the Four C's of Consciousness, Chemicals, Cosmetics and Creativity as necessary components of the Art of Creative Suffering. If the readers perform the activities we suggest, they will undoubtedly find great relief from major hangover pain.

CHAPTER THREE: THE MEDIA—DISTRACTED FROM DISTRACTION BY DISTRACTION

This chapter is the first of the next four that offers specific creative remedies for the distracted consciousness of the hangover victim. It suggests a variety of movies and television programs so compelling that hangover victims will be distracted from their condition. It also points out a range of actors and actresses whose charisma, charm and humor will undoubtedly sooth frazzled nerves (i.e., the Commanding Presence of Claude Rains, the Forgiving Mother of Jane Darwell, the silliness of Carmen Miranda and Dr. Watson, etc.). The chapter concludes with an annotated listing of the twenty most highly recommended films and television shows to watch with a hangover and an additional listing of what television programs to avoid (i.e., NOVA specials on autopsy, old episodes of Dobie Gillis, etc.).

CHAPTER 4: FROM MUSE-SICK TO MUSIC

This chapter deals, as in the previous one, with creative remedies for Hangover agony, but from a musical point of view. The Muses (those creative elements of the imagination) have been seriously damaged during last night's over-indulgence, thus the Muses are sick (musick!). As a curative we offer an annotated listing of not only the kind of music to listen to, but suggest specific musical selections from a wide range of classical, popular, jazz, country and western, and rock music to help soothe hangover jitters. We offer the reader a model in preparing their own 90-minute tape to be readily available for treatment of their next serious hangover. Most important, we match the piece with the severity of the discomfort, i.e., Bach's *"Come, Sweet Death!"* for particularly bad mornings.

CHAPTER 5: THE READING READINESS TEST

This chapter concentrates on helping the hangover victim begin to take guarded steps to approaching some kind of reading activity. We suggest beginning with large photograph books, map reading, Almanacs, and dictionaries with illustrations (i.e., *The American Heritage Dictionary)* and moving slowly into the seven best novelists to read with a hangover (i.e., Lawrence Sanders, G.K. Chesterton, Simenon, etc.). We point out four classic hangover scenes that are genuinely funny (Peter Fallow "coming to" in Tom Wolfe's *Bonfire of the Vanities*) and conclude with the Literary Master of the Hangover, poet and novelist, Charles Bukowski. We advocate self-irony rather than self-pity in our readings.

CHAPTER 6: EXORCISE WITH EXERCISE—IMAGINATIVE CALISTHENICS

Beginning with the premise that "exercise" is the best form of "exorcism" (that is, driving out the evil spirits of the night before), we propose a series of activities that will act as a cure for the condition such as mixing media (i.e., paging through Norman Rockwell sketches while listening to Aaron Copland's ballet music), or combining Map Reading with music and history (i.e., Smetana's *The Moldau*). We also suggest limited physical activity such as conducting a phantom symphony orchestra or performing piano concertos on the coffee table. Other activities include initiating Hangover Support Groups, consciously inventing your own world and other quasi-cultural, New Age self-help activities.

CHAPTER 7: THE ST. LAWRENCE MEMORIAL RECIPE—STATIONS OF THE COURSE

St. Lawrence is the patron saint of hangover victims because he was literally fried to death over hot coals in third century Rome. You, on the other hand, were metaphorically fried last night by your poison of choice. Here, we summarize and offer the ultimate hangover remedy recipe.

AN AFTERWORD TO THE WISE

A brief bit of advice for people who are hung over on a regular basis and whose drinking may be approaching the stage where it's getting to be a drag for them and everybody else. Light but to the point.

PREFACE
"WHAT'S COOKIN...?"—YOUR BRAINS OR YOUR IMAGINATION?

In his classic work, *On Drink*, the distinguished British novelist and essayist, Sir Kingsley Amis, divides the hangover condition into two parts: "the physical and the metaphysical." Our little volume deals directly with the effects of the "physical hangover" by recommending over seventy specific menus for the "day after." In addition, it offers healing treatments for the "metaphysical hangover" in its many and various manifestations.

We use the term "cookbook" as it applies not only to an activity that takes place in the actual kitchen of your home but, more importantly, as a psychological, mental, and spiritual "kitchen" in which the imagination does the cooking. When someone pops in the doorway and asks: "Hey, what's cookin'?" they are not interested in food preparation, but rather in "what's going on, what's taking place, what's happening?" in the kitchen of your imagination. When Jazz artists lose themselves in the act of improvisation and the music takes over, it's called: "Puttin' on the Pots!" Since the imagination is, obviously, a kitchen in which we "cook up" ideas, schemes, plans, and remedies for both "physical" and "metaphysical" hangovers, we are employing the word, "cookbook," in its widest and most generic sense. And, since present-day "consumption" comprises not just food and drink but also media of diverse kinds, we offer gentle guidance in choices of music, film, literature and televised spectacle—imaginative "food"—to ameliorate the effects of overindulgence of other substances.

THE EXISTENTIAL DILEMMA AND BEFUDDLEMENT

Over and above the painful effects of both the "physical" and "metaphysical" hangover, there is the added befuddlement of choice. Hangover victims literally do not know what to do, the heart of most dilemmas. The enormous range of choices simply paralyzes them into a state of inertia. Indeed, the word, "befuddle," specifically refers to a condition of confusion directly related to overindulgence in alcohol. In fact, one of the

American Heritage Dictionary definitions of the word is: "to stupify with alcoholic drink." This little book proposes to tell them exactly what to do, to direct the healing energies of their imagination and focus them on the kinds of activities that will release them from the befuddlement of their over-cooked brains.

THE ART OF CREATIVE SUFFERING

Most importantly, though, is that all of our remedies, treatments, and exercises participate in what we have designated the Art of Creative Suffering. The energy to "cure" the hangover must come from within ourselves; that is, the creative potential which this little book will help generate.

Chapter 1: The Wrath of Grapes

Morning Dread and What Not to Do

The "morning after" should be re-named the "mourning after" to better capture the agony following the ecstasy of the night before. Regrettably, you have completely forgotten the ecstasy. The sunlight flowing through the window upon your wounded body is creating the same effect as it always did on Dracula, only you don't, unfortunately, begin to melt into green goo, which would be a relief at this stage. You peer down at your decimated body, astonished that you were actually able to get it in the bed and your P.J.'s relatively unscathed.

Now great waves of dread begin to activate the guilt as tiny half images of remembrance filter through the outer parameters of your quivering consciousness. "Oh, no, I didn't say that, did I? To my boss? Oh, no—worse yet—it's coming back: I told that filthy joke to his wife!"

And now you have arrived, overwhelmed with self-loathing and entertaining suicidal notions, at the place where another drink could shut down those Memories from Hell. However, the first and most important rule in attending to your hangover pain is this: DON'T START DRINKING AGAIN (the Hair of the Dog routine) because that's not treating the hangover. It's a continuation of the drunk. And in spite of feeling biodegradable and seriously thinking that you're living in an Edgar Allan Poe story, drinking destroys any possibility of dealing with the condition. Continuing the drunk becomes a massive failure of the imagination, and precludes the only source available to you now: the energy of the imagination, the creative force. Remember Luke Skywalker's: "May the Force be with you?" Well, it's the same one.

Now for the most of you, even the thought of drinking the next morning will have approximately the same effect as the Dracula Sunlight Syndrome; that is, formally vowing that you will never touch that stuff again! Well, at least for a very long time, anyway.

But the major problem of the Hangover can be simply stated: How do I get through the day, salvage it? How do I handle the anxiety, the existential dread that could be with me for at least twelve hours? This book is about creative suffering and how to use that pain to invent a tolerable, productive, interesting and, maybe, enjoyable day.

You can accomplish this Herculean task in spite of a frazzled nervous system by plugging into and availing yourself of the energies of guilt. Actually, a lot of modern American and British literature was written with hangovers and the accompanying guilt. One of America's permanently hung over writers, Dorothy Parker, epitomized perfectly the hangover condition in her classic admission after a dedicated night of two-fisted drinking with her fellow New Yorker cronies: "My nerves are so bad today I'd cry over card tricks." But then she and her drinking buddies at the Algonquin Hotel wrote some of the wittiest stories of the modern era. "Hangover Guilt" is one of Western civilization's great, unrecognized creative energy sources. Ernest Hemingway, William Faulkner, F. Scott Fitzgerald, Thomas Wolfe, Sinclair Lewis, James Joyce, John Cheever, Ray Carver, and Barry Hannah and many other writers suffered from what the Irish call "Boozer's Gloom," but they channeled that pain into creating fictions for us to enjoy. Our Chapter V on what to read with a hangover will detail their accomplishments as well as suggest other appropriate readings.

Caring for the Body: Speech and Hearing Problems

Because the synapses of our brains have been radically derailed into startlingly strange paths, it's crucial not to act intuitively. Dionysus, the god of ecstatic orgy, ruled last night; but Apollo, the god of reason and intelligence, must take over this morning. Speaking, even mouthing words could be difficult, and coherent conversation will come only with great effort. You may become unusually dismayed to hear yourself uttering Dan Quayle fear-of-preposition-like sentences such as: "Darling, could you call in please the orifice of the boss that I'm can't come in today to work now please!" Or you may hear yourself pronouncing two and sometimes three words at once, and generally having a real hard time making yourself understood. Kind (un-hung-over) people will usually ask you to repeat yourself. Don't let their smug sobriety put you off. Even though some of them will be genuinely sympathetic, you'll tend to consider anybody sober the next day quite virtuous. Their simplest assertions will sound like moral directives from some television evangelist dripping with self-congratulation. Your feelings of guilt will transform the merely sober into unctuous, annoying harpies who "really" know all the details of your drunken excesses of the night before, or so you paranoiacally suspect. Therefore, be on your guard. You were struck partially dumb by last night's overindulgence, and you also can't hear very well. Because of your partial deafness, most of what you do hear will seem sad and pointless. The "sober ones" who conscientiously try to follow your fractured conversation might even begin to talk like you and run the risk of becoming similarly befuddled. So listen; don't try to talk.

GUILTY MOUTH SYNDROME

Because of the super-sensitivity of both the nervous system and your moral conscience, the mouth and what may have come out of it or, worse yet, what may have gone into it, will begin to cause serious problems. Great anxiety comes from the mind's inability to remember important details. But the body, unable to articulate in words or images, but remembering everything, responds as if you were the captain of the Exxon Valdez and soiled an entire coastline during your drunken revelries of the previous evening. The mouth, unfortunately, has a memory and, as an aperture, might give you difficulties beyond mere word formulation. This condition is called "guilty mouth syndrome," and will seem to have "things" in it. Small, fuzzy "things," like cob-webs, only less definite. Much of the day will be spent trying to get them out, and men with beards and mustaches will endlessly pull at their mouths. This continuous "being at your mouth" might disturb normal people and frustrate the kind ones who would like to assist, but feel helpless and even silly asking if they can help you get whatever it is in your mouth out of it. So give those around you a break and go off somewhere alone to pull at your mouth.

MIRROR, MIRROR: OR THE VISINE VISION

Vision, too, is sometimes impaired. Remember, things are not what they seem on those vulnerable mornings, thanks to whatever gods there may be! The well-scrubbed face of the cheerful paperboy may seem like some angst-ridden, bodiless cherub out of a Grunewald painting or a Stephen King novel; and the perceptual field will resemble an exhausted film, green lines oscillating spastically with savage irregularity. And what we can envision will seem, peripherally, out of an early Ingmar Bergman film: dour, dusky, and slightly threatening. Quickly opening the eyes can produce a condition of radical astonishment: we actually do exist after last night! Harold Arlen's "The Man Who Got Away" floats mercifully into the fragmented consciousness of a regularly hung-over friend and accompanies his guarded search for the brutally fluorescent bathroom.

Once in the bathroom, the task of extricating those same "things" that were in your mouth from your eyes (remember "guilty mouth syndrome"?) will begin. This is called "guilty eyes syndrome." Frustrating attempts may continue throughout the day, relentlessly blinking your eyes to get "them" out. If it was a particularly bad night, you'll find yourself using fingers first, then palms and backs of hands, and finally knuckles to work on your eyes. The knuckles are the best because of the variety of safe surfaces coming partially into your eyes and fully onto the lids. The pathetic alcoholic recidivist, Freddy Malins in James Joyce's "The Dead" is a prime example of someone trying to get those "things" out of his eyes. But here, again, this chronic exertion may begin to bother your normal friends. It's like watching a television special on "Insects"; everybody begins to get itchy. They unconsciously mimic your motions, and the next thing you know everybody is at their eyes trying to get "them" out, like infants bunching their little fists into their eyes just before sleep. Again, work on your eyes in private, like you did with your mouth.

One of the few genuinely comic movie scenes in which the Hangover is treated with brutal directness comes from that very entertaining film *15 Minutes,* a film the critics didn't appreciate enough. Robert De Niro plays a heavy drinking celebrity NYPD cop named Eddie Fleming who loves his weekly fifteen minutes of fame on Kelsey Grammer's talk show. When Grammer's boss objects to Fleming's excessive drinking, Grammer casually states: "He's found a cure for that." The next scene shows De Niro plunging his entire head into a bathtub full of ice water, then pulling it out, obviously traumatized but clearly sobered up or, at least, hangover free. We do not recommend this technique, especially for those with weak hearts. The scene concludes with De Niro drenching his bloodshot eyes with, we presume, Visine and beginning a new day beaming with confidence. In viewing the film recently, there is little doubt that the two immigrant murderers from eastern Europe are very, *very* hungover. Check 'em out! I don't mean the characters; I mean the actors themselves. By the way, my former student, Ed Burns, co-stars, and he and De Niro work together beautifully.

CARING FOR THE MIND: DON'T SPEAK, MEMORY! OR, LOOKING FOR MR. LOBOTOMY

One of your urges may be to start calling up people you were drinking with the night before and ask them if you actually did or said some of the stupid things you, hopefully, only dreamt you did. *Resist that urge.* You are feeling lots of guilt in your present condition, so don't make it worse. If you are home for the day, it would not be wise to get out your old high school year books and run the risk of a nostalgia attack. Your condition has made you extremely vulnerable to any emotions, especially those that memories of the happy past may evoke. And you run the risk, if you're still a bit buzzed, of actually calling up your old steady from your teen years which could really push you over the edge, particularly when they have completely forgotten who you are.

Keep in mind that the project of this book is to enable you to create imaginative possibilities that can get you through the day. A heavy dose of nostalgia may thwart the creative edge of the imagination and runs the risk of fixating you on your pain rather than your potential. Here is a list of some additional activities that would be best to avoid:

Don't visit the Zoo. The erratic and absolutely unpredictable behavior of the animals may seriously disturb you. Avoid at all costs the Monkey House which will validate the ancient, but alarmingly modern Chinese proverb: "My life is a drunken monkey!" And their poor little red butts will shatter your nervous system and may evoke sympathetic pain from your own backside. Whatever you do, if you must take the kids to the Zoo, stay away from the reptile and insect houses. No explanation is needed here.

Don't study the physical habits of your pets, especially the dog. Cats are mercifully enigmatic and won't evoke too much paranoid response from you, although their piercing stare could unnerve you if you observe too long. Dogs, however, especially their incredibly quick eyebrow movements, should be avoided. Their eyebrow activity may pull you into the emotions that they seem to be expressing and will exhaust your mind by trying to follow their quickly changing feelings from sadness-to-happiness-to-fear-to-illness-to-daffiness, and so on *ad infinitum.* This is called "dog's eyes syndrome." It's the old problem of what poets call the "pathetic fallacy"; that is, projecting human emotions into simple animal actions that mean nothing—which is really pathetic. Their eyebrows are probably adjusting to light refraction since most dogs are half blind anyway and they're simply trying to see you. But don't think about that too much, either.

Don't watch television shows which feature song writers who try to sing their own songs. They usually can't play the piano very well and none of them can sing at all, so you'll be spending your time and energy hitting the right notes for them while simultaneously trying to adjust your ears to their off-key singing. Although Marvin Hamlisch, the renowned composer of the music for *A Chorus Line* and other great shows, can play the piano quite well, his singing is excruciating. He also looks like the loan officer who just vetoed your mortgage application, so the mixture of the beauty of his songs with the banker banality of his appearance and off-key singing might create serious nerve damage.

Don't watch puppet shows especially those that indulge in

vicious beatings, the kind where an incredibly ugly puppet tries to pulverize an even uglier puppet into silence. Kids love "Punch and Judy Shows," but they're not suffering a hangover.

Don't go to high school band concerts. While there is much pleasure to be derived from listening to teenagers play as loud as they can (have you ever heard a *subtle* high school band?), the sheer animal energy roaring off the stage at you in your condition could really push you over the edge.

Don't watch television evangelists (the few who are left) hysterically declaiming on the wages of sin, the Second Coming, the Rapture and demanding "Amens." And beware of heartbreaking hymns like "Amazing Grace," especially its reference to "a wretch like me" which may describe how you feel in your hung-over condition.

Don't ever watch Amateur Talent shows for obvious reasons. The unique brand of embarrassment they can evoke could become lethal. The typical killer entertainer from this masochistic enterprise is the garishly dressed accordion player from Cleveland, Ohio, ripping through "Lady of Spain" triple speed with close-ups on both his whirling spangled speakers and ring-covered hands that rival Liberace for bad taste. Worse than the sparkling hands are those players, usually from Detroit, who perform "Malagena" with black leather gloves through a thick Turkish towel. Go back to bed! The most embarrassing amateur performers ever recorded, however, were twin teenage boys from Smoot, West Virginia (who looked *exactly* alike) roller skating to a Temptations' record!

Don't even go near Mexican music or any music from Central or South America because of its excessive busyness. It could tear you apart because your ears will not be able to follow any one musical line of development or rhythmic pattern. An extended discussion of this peculiar brand of musical frenzy can be seen in Chapter IV: "From Muse-sick to Music."

We shall now proceed to the next chapter which will be a listing and discussion of simple non-alcoholic medical remedies. Remember the premise of this book is that intake of alcohol in any form is a continuation of the drunk and a massive failure of the imagination, your only friend when hung over. We propose a variety of recipes to treat both the "physical" and "metaphysical" hangover and to show you how to employ your imagination in combating the effects of over-indulgence in alcohol. The following chapters will define precisely what constitutes a hangover and offer some safe remedies for head-aches, queasy stomachs, and jangled nerves.

Of course, our first and most obvious remedy for both "physical" and "metaphysical" hangover pain in any form is the reading and enjoyment of this book which has been specifical-ly tailored to meet those needs.

We will conclude each chapter with specific food recipes under the six food/beverage categories listed below:

    I. BEVERAGES & SOUPS or "B&S"
   II. MEATS, POULTRY & EGGS or "MP&E"
  III. FISH & SHELLFISH or "F&S"
  IV. VEGETABLES & SALADS or "V&S"
   V. FRUITS or "F"
 VI. DESSERTS or "D"

MENU

"B&S"

1. An ancient Irish Folk Cure recommended by one of Ireland's most distinguished Folklore experts, Michael J. Murphy. You must use ice cold spring water (this has nothing to do with the soap Irish Spring!). Throw in a handful of oats and mix gingerly. Then quaff it down very quickly and, according to legend, you'll feel relief in about 15 minutes.

2. Drink ice cold water, as much as possible, until your head hurts. Alcohol dehydrates the body radically.

3. Sermons and Soda Water: George Gordon, Lord Byron, great English satirist was the one Romantic poet who drank heavily and suffered accordingly:

> *Few things surpass old wine; and they*
>   *may preach*
> *Who please—the more because they*

> *preach in vain—*
> *Let us have Wine and Women, Mirth*
>   *and Laughter,*
> *Sermons and Soda water—the day after …*
> *Man, being reasonable, must*
>   *get drunk;*
> *The best of life is but*
>   *Intoxication …*
> *Get very drunk and when*
> *You wake with head-ache,*
> *You shall see what then.*
> *Ring for your valet—bid him quickly*
>   *bring*
> *Some hock★ and soda-water, then*
>   *you'll know*
> *A pleasure worthy of Xerxes the great*
>   *king.*

Lord Byron, *Don Juan,* Book II, Canto II, Stanzas: 178-79

★Leave the "hock" out, because it's a white Rhine wine. 'Member, no alcohol!

4. A milk shake, particularly vanilla or chocolate. Our four-star second most highly recommended elixir, after gazpacho (see page 122), is a very thick chocolate or vanilla milk shake with whole wheat toast drenched in butter or margarine, and a tiny bit of garlic salt sprinkled across the toast.

5. Onion soup served with lots of parmesan and Swiss cheese melted on top; it should be accompanied with garlic bread also with browned parmesan cheese spread over it and lightly sprinkled with garlic salt.

"MP&E"

1. Sweet and Sour Pork or Chicken of any kind. The mixture of sweet and sour somehow soothes the taste buds of the hangover victim as does no other food.

2. Chinese food of almost any kind, but soak it with plenty of soy sauce or teriyaki sauce. Shrimp rolls are very appeal-

ing but be careful with the dumplings; their quivering may bother the squeamish.

3. A southern Ohio cousin, Billy Joe Yoho, claimed that the following recipe would create such gustative ecstasy that you would virtually forget you had a hangover: Pork chops dipped in honey, soy sauce, and a little mustard and grilled on an outdoor grill if possible. These are best if marinated overnight. The honey should be darkened with the soy sauce and mixed with yellow mustard. If you have tears, prepare to shed them!

"V&S"

1. The Seamus Heaney (renowned Irish Poet and Nobel Prize Winner) Northern Irish Hangover Cure—Champ: Mashed potatoes mixed with tons of butter, cream, and onions with a glass of ice-cold milk.

2. Fried rice mixed with mushrooms, onions, cashews, butter, soy sauce, and served with an ice cold glass of milk.

"F"

1. Peaches and cream with lots of sugar or sugar substitute.

2. The Jim Morrison Hangover Cure: An entire ice-cold watermelon sprinkled with lots of salt. Bury your feverish face in it for maximum results.

"D"

As much vanilla ice cream as possible (Ben & Jerry's or Häagen Dazs)

Chapter Two: More Wrath

The Need for a Comprehensive Hangover Cookbook and What *to* Do

The need for a Comprehensive or complete Hangover Cookbook is clear. Over the years much literature on drink and drinking has appeared. Books abound on the art of mixing drinks, on what wine to drink with what food, the social history of drinking, how to throw a successful cocktail (whatever that is) party, and even, oddly enough, on how drinking may benefit your health. Most of this stuff is written by people who don't address the larger issues and whose imagination is limited by their overly specific pet interests.

Drink books proliferate and attempt to make the occasional drinker a connoisseur, a minor expert, in one particular area of alcohol. But usually these attempts prove impractical and become mere book collector's items at best. And we insist, in our book, that alcohol must never be used as a "so-called" cure.

Similarly, another body of literature dedicates itself mainly to condemning drink. Volumes (especially government pamphlets) abound on "alcohol abuse." Long studies will show us how millions of industrial dollars are lost annually because workers tend to miss Mondays or do not fully awaken to their tasks until Tuesday afternoon around 3 P.M.

But the subject of the hangover itself is neglected. Where can you find serious, sensible, and imaginative information on why hangovers occur at all? or how to treat them? or even how to avoid them? Probably nowhere but in this little book, although an intelligent and witty book called *The Hangover Handbook*, written by David Outerbridge, was published about ten years ago. Until now, no handy compilation of remedies which cover the physical and metaphysical hangover was available to combat and help relieve its effects or what we have imaginatively (we hope!) re-defined as the "Wrath of Grapes." Get it?

In fact, so little attention has been paid to the hangover that the best dictionaries do not define the word correctly!

Therefore, this book, we hope, should prove, pardon the pun, definitive. All facts, recipes, observations, and suggestions have been carefully researched and documented. The sources are wide-ranging, including classical and current, mythical and scientific. Our comprehensive or holistic cookbook includes advice from diverse sources ranging from scientific and medical journals to poets, novelists, musicians and even bartenders.

A PROPER DEFINITION OF HANGOVER

The subject of the hangover has been so ignored, for whatever reasons, that the best dictionaries never take the word seriously or bother to define it correctly. Take for example the vague and moralistically loaded definitions longstanding in the following sources:

"The unpleasant after-effects of dissipation," *The Oxford English Dictionary*.

"The effect of a period of dissipation after the exhilaration has worn off" (United States slang), *Webster's New International Dictionary*.

"Unpleasant physical effects following the heavy use of alcohol," *American Heritage New College Dictionary*.

"The headache following the overindulgence in alcoholic liquor" (informal), *Funk and Wagnalls Standard College Dictionary*.

"Unpleasant physical effects following the heavy use of alcohol," *The American Heritage Dictionary of the English Language* (Fourth edition).

"The disagreeable physical after-effects of drunkenness, usually felt several hours after cessation of drinking," *Random House Dictionary*.

"The morning after the night before," (circa, 1910). Eric Partridge, *A Dictionary of Slang and Unconventional English*.

A much more accurate definition is one offered by Dr. Benjamin Karpman, M.D., whose 531-page volume entitled *The Hangover* constitutes the only serious book-length treatment and discussion to date of the condition: "A hangover is a physical and emotional state caused by, and following, the excessive use of alcohol... the unpleasant and undesirable, sometimes very painful, after-effects of which the individual is conscious following any excessive indulgence." Dr. Karpman laments the fact that most psychiatric textbooks and dictionaries simply leave the word out, and that the first ten volumes of the *Quarterly Journal of Studies on Alcohol* rarely mentions the word at all.

But anyone who has experienced a hangover knows that not one of these definitions, with the exception of Dr. Karpman's, is accurate. After all, "dissipation" connotes outright moral irresponsibility and wasteful destructiveness—certainly a reckless, self-indulgent intemperance, at best. Yet, studies show that a hangover may result from a mere drink or two, or an attitude of mind while having a few drinks, or even the atmosphere of a particular drinking place.

Furthermore, hangover is strictly a 20th-century American word, so we shouldn't rely on bluenoses or scholars who compile dictionaries to define it for us. Except for Karpman, all those definitions overlook fully one half of the effects of alcohol, namely, the mental and psychological unpleasantness that regularly results from a hangover. Therefore, we define the word accurately and without undue moralizing:

Hangover: "The temporary disagreeable physical and metaphysical effects that generally follow drinking," *The Wrath of Grapes.*

Before World War I, the word was rarely used to describe the after-effects of alcohol. However, it gained prominence and became fashionable in American usage in the 1920's, and especially during prohibition. Hemingway used it frequently. But the connotation of bad effects, resulting from alcohol overconsumption harks back to our very national roots focusing on a stigma connected with any kind of association with alcohol. Although George Washington made corn liquor himself, he said that whiskey would "ruin half the workmen in this country." And John Adams, not a teetotaler, lamented, "Is it not mortifying that we Americans should exceed all other people in the world in this degrading, beastly vice of intemperance?" Degrading or not, Americans still drink more liquor and beer combined than any other nation in the world. At present, there are 90 million Americans who drink!

The American word "hangover," as properly defined, describes the total result of drinking too much as no equivalent words in other languages do. Modern European languages often provide the roots of American and English vocabulary, but not in the case of hangover.

For example, the French regularly drink vast quantities of wine and of course experience "mourning's after"—oops— "mornings after." Yet their linguistic description of what they feel is quite understated and special, though they sometimes use the word, "hangover." Their words do not have the blank-check effect of our all-embracing word accurately and without undue moralizing onomatopoetic description. In French, to have a hangover, is rendered colloquially, *avoir la gueule de bois,* "to have a wooden mouth, a mouth dry as wood," Nice. But surely on occasion a few Frenchmen have drunk enough to incur more hangover pain and horror than simple dry mouth suggests. We have re-named this condition as "guilty-mouth syndrome" and described its symptoms in Chapter One.

Spaniards also consume lots of wine, yet they are slightly more inclusive in their familiar term to describe the condition of hangover. *Tener resaca,* that is, "to be presently experiencing effects as a result of a previous condition," or roughly, "to have a backwash of bad effects." But inhabitants of sunny countries don't seem to have as many hangovers as those who live in gloomy, northern climates.

While the Spanish translation for "hangover" may be adequate for a nation that does not attempt to import and consume every kind of liquor the world produces, as Americans try to do, most other Mediterranean vocabularies are equally barren of a descriptive word for hangover. The Greeks don't have one though Zorba drank regularly. And in truth, the Italians, second only to the French in the consumption of wine, also do not have an adequate word for hangover. Oh,

Italian-American dictionaries try to construct neat little phrases for tourists to convey the meaning, such as *mal di capo dopo una bevuta* (isn't that awful?) or, "my head hurts after a drinking bout"; not an overwhelmingly clever idiom yet about as dully literal as movie titles such as *She's Having a Baby!* But many of our Italian friends simply use the American term.

However, the Germans, long known for their ability to drink beer, wine, and stronger stuff, have a neat, colorful word for hangover: *Katzenjammer*. Middle-aged American readers of comic strips will recall Hans, Fritz, and der Captain of "Der Katzenjammer Kids," dear to our hearts for over forty years. Katzenjammer is composed of two German words, *Katzen*-cats, and *jammer*—a verb meaning "to lament or to cry." So having a hangover in Germany is to hear numerous cats yowling in your cranium.

The Norwegians (reputed to be able to out-drink even the Germans) replace cats in the cranium with *Jeg har tommermenn!*—"I have carpenters in my head."

The Poles and other bordering nations use variations of the German term. *Katza* is a shortened Polish equivalent. Could one of the reasons for such a glaring linguistic vacuum be a subtle form of denial? We found it curious that so very few precise words exist to describe the condition even in heavy-drinking cultures.

The most curious word for hangover that we came across was the Serbo-Croatian *mamurluk*. It shares the same etymological root as the word *mameluk* meaning "a slave," and the Arabic *mamluk* meaning "a thing owned." The Egyptians indentured enormous numbers of *Mamelukes* from central Asia as slaves during the Middle Ages. The hangover, then, is viewed as a form of slavery by the Serbo-Croatians. *Mamurluk* also means "seedy, maudlin, and crapulous."

And speaking of "crapulous," the Romans used the Latin word *crapula* to denote "intoxication and drunkenness"; while the Greeks, always a little sharper and more precise, used the earlier root of that word *(kraipale)* to also mean "a debauch and its consequences: nausea, headache, and hangover." Thus the English word *crapulence*; that is, sickness caused by excessive eating or drinking. We speculate, then, that our slang word "crappy" specifically refers to the hangover as it affects the lower intestines for the next several days.

KINDS OF DRINKS AND THE HANGOVER—BEWARE THE MARTINI

Although the hangover itself often comes as a surprise to its victim, no one who has ever experienced the condition doubts that its effects are both physically and metaphysically devastating. Usually the debilitation to one's system caused from drinking occurs in a rough proportion to the amount and kind of alcohol consumed. Untreated, a hangover can last from 16-40 hours! The little chart that follows attempts to provide a general scale, showing the strength of typical drinks quaffed by average imbibers. At this point, keep in mind that proof (alcoholic strength of a drink) can be important when considering the number of drinks taken. This table of equivalents is based upon volume and proof, and is important when considering potency of drinks. Of course, many other factors will bear upon the intensity of any hangover resulting from the kinds of drinks you down. We are not talking about effect yet.

THE RELATIVE ALCOHOLIC STRENGTH OF LIQUOR, BEER, AND WINE, ROUGHLY CALCULATED:

(Powerful Drinks)

1 large dry gin (94 proof) or Vodka (100 proof) Martini (including negligible amount of 38 proof dry vermouth)	=	2 large (80 proof) blended whiskey Manhattan(s) 4 03 (including 1 oz. 32 proof sweet vermouth)

(Strong Drinks)

three 1 oz. (80 proof) Seagrams 7 shots of blended whiskey with short (3 oz) beer chaser (9 proof)	=	3 1/2 1 oz. shots of (86 proof) Cutty Sark scotch on ice with a splash of water

(Normal Drinks)

four 12 oz. glasses of domestic beer (9 proof)	=	or three five-ounce goblets burgundy wine (25 proof)

And so on…

Clearly, the high proof, dry Martini is the most powerful common drink known to mankind—and also one of the most popular. This lethal weapon contains three ounces of almost pure 94 proof gin or 100 proof vodka, if you would rather call it a "gimlet." The blended whiskey in a Manhattan is only 80 proof and the volume of alcohol less, for any decent Manhattan must contain almost 1/3 sweet vermouth. However, the dry Martini usually carries only a whisper of dry vermouth. Even so, dry vermouth registers 36 proof, while sweet is somewhat weaker at 32 proof–perhaps an inconsequential statistic over the long pull.

But the strength of the Martini should not be underestimated. Most bars and restaurants that serve good food and drink make huge, dry ones. Even on the rocks, which palliates them some, Martinis can carry a lot of gin. Measure one sometime at your favorite luncheon spa or check your own freely-poured-before-dinner Martini at home to be totally unsurprised why you feel so done-in every night before ten.

Naturally, it is not uncommon for a Martini drinker to have two before a meal. And since inflation has caught up with everything, the businessman's Martini Lunch may now be a 3-M Lunch. Such quick, high-proof alcoholic intake—say six ounces or more—before eating, guarantees a more than slight buzz in most imbibers and an afternoon at the office that will produce nothing but mindless paper shuffling.

Ordinary drinks usually consist of an ounce of liquor, diluted by ice and three to six ounces of mixer or water. Naturally the effect of such a highball (as silly a word as "cocktail") is less. It's easy to see that downing three tall scotch and sodas—a quite unappetizing trick before meals—would have less effect on a drinker than a well-made, straight-up Martini.

WHITE LIQUOR OR BROWN, CONGENERS, EFFERVESCENCE

Martinis made with vodka, which can come in higher proof than even the strongest gins, are also more powerful than other drinks. But vodka may be expected to do more than leave you "breathless." Tests undertaken by Kent State researchers show that drinking 100 proof vodka can lead to higher highs and more exaggerated actions than would drinking bourbon, for instance. Vodka is absorbed into the blood faster than equal amounts of bourbon over the same period of time. Moreover, the vodka drinkers proved to be more aggressive and anxious than the bourbon drinkers. Other experiments conducted at the University of California suggest that a more severe hangover results from drinking bourbon as compared to vodka or gin. Gin and vodka are purer than "brown" or colored whiskies and contain fewer congeners. Scientists have long suggested that the congeners—organic alcohols, salts, fused oils, coloring and aging additives—present in most alcohol cured in wood (bourbon, scotch, and some ryes, whiskies, and wines) account for the intensity of hangover. In fact, it is the lack of congeners in vodka that leaves drinkers' breath free of smell. But by and large the kind—and amount—of drink one takes surely contributes to the "quality" of one's day after.

For example, a carbonated or effervescent mixer will get the alcohol into your blood a lot quicker than will plain water or no mixer at all. Any water will dilute the alcohol and slow its absorption. But soda water (and ginger ale) hurries the drink into the bloodstream faster. Rapid absorption accounts for quick intoxication. So without doubt, the effects of Scotch and soda are quicker than Scotch and water or Scotch on the rocks. It follows like the day the night, then, that quaffing copious shots and beers, a very potent effervescent combo, will make short work of even a hearty, experienced drinker.

Likewise, the compliment paid the lover in the old song, "You go to my head like champagne," is sincere. Bubbly, sparkling wines of any kind rush alcohol to the small intestines, zip it into the bloodstream, where it rapidly moves to the brain and works on the old imagination. Still wines are much slower all around. And just as gin and vodka have fewer impurities and congeners than bourbon, scotch or other aged, colored, and flavored whiskies, so too has white wine fewer impurities than red.

Most commercial wines are not simple and pure, but contain hundred of chemical compounds (if all the ingredients of wine were listed on labels, supplementary bottles might have to be issued!) High on the list of impurities in red wines is an abundance of histamines. Some experts associate histamines, which are found in plant and animal tissue, with allergy and headache. A straight beer hangover, however, can be more punishing than one resulting from either liquor or wine. Beer has a greater food value (especially carbohydrates) which tends to slow absorption of alcohol into the blood, stretching out the period of drunkenness. It is a good deal lower in proof than whiskey, too.

And since beer is not thought to be as powerful as liquor or wine, it deceives drinkers into thinking they can handle a good deal of it without getting as drunk as a whiskey drinker or a wine "connoisseur." Not so. While it may take longer for a beer drinker's blood to reach the same point of alcoholic saturation as a whiskey drinker's, the alcohol from beer will remain in the system longer, and the beer hangover will "hang around" longer too. Beer is carbonated, and carbonated beverages can work for or against you, depending on your condition as they aid alcohol in entry into the bloodstream.

HANGOVER IS ACTION: A COMBINATION OF PHYSICAL AND MENTAL FACTORS

In any case, a hangover is a result of several immediate factors: How many drinks have you actually taken? What proof alcohol did you drink? Normally 90% of alcohol is oxidized by the liver and almost completely absorbed into the blood and dissipated at the rate of one drink every hour and a half. Little or no alcohol is sweated out or breathed out. So, theoretically, if you drink slowly enough, you won't feel it—while drinking or after. How slow? Well, by making each can of beer last about an hour-and-a-half. Or by sipping your scotch and water for the same amount of time.

Quantity, alcoholic proof, and rate of consumption are only a partial measure of the kind and intensity of any hangover that may await you. Personal drinking qualifications also apply such as sex, age, weight, frame of mind and gender.

The old generalization that men hold their liquor better than women is probably true, but only for basic physical reasons. The bodies of men contain an average of 10-15% more fluid than women's bodies—which gives the male an edge in diluting alcohol. And because the average man weighs more than the average woman, his body distributes drink over a greater area of blood supply, arteries, capillaries, etc.; in short, a heavy person is a little less affected by drink than a lightweight.

However, the difference in capacity due to one's bulk can be small. For example, after six drinks (other than devastating martinis, of course) in a period of two hours, the blood alcohol content of a person weighing 120 pounds would probably show intoxication in the legal sense. At the same time, the blood of someone weighing as much as 200 pounds would show the very same result after only one more drink!

Of course, the systems of young drinkers will metabolize (get rid of) alcohol faster than old timers. Naturally, as we age, the body processes we take pride in, slow down remorselessly.

Even when well-aware of your own physicality, how much you are drinking, how strong the drink, how fast the drinks are coming—in other words how carefully you try to avoid overdoing–you may awake, after a very short sleep, to find the hangover has slipped through all your carefully constructed defenses.

Earlier, we suggested that for some incredible reason drinkers rarely expect to be hung over next day, no matter how often they have experienced the ill-effects of alcohol in the past. No one ever wittingly welcomes a hangover into his bedroom. When it strikes, the victim remains surprised by all of its effects and vaguely insulted, while he endures the physical and mental attack that ensues.

The painful physical results of a serious hangover outnumber the metaphysical agonies about two-to-one, although the sufferer doesn't necessarily think them more grave. Shakespeare described the special, classic results of drinking almost 400 years ago in Macbeth:

> Porter: Faith, sir, we are carousing … and drink, sir, is a great
> provoker of three things.
> Macduff: What three things does drink especially provoke?
> Porter: Marry, sir, nose-painting, sleep, and urine. Lechery, sir, it
> provokes and unprovokes. It provokes the desire, but it
> takes away the performance.

While the obvious physical results described by the Bard are unimpeachable, his opinion of alcohol's influence on sexual capability has been debated over the years. Whether or not drink is an anti-aphrodisiac or not often depends on individual propensities. Some medical evidence does suggest that the ingestion of any alcohol decreases the production of testosterone (male hormone) in "normal" men. And Shakespeare's observations on red noses and diuresis (copious urination) as a result of drinking have long been supported by research. But any definitive statement on the effects of hangover should point out that the immediate or short-term results are always temporary.

In fact, we have classified a conglomerate of the Physical and Metaphysical (psychological, spiritual in many cases) effects of hangover for easy reference. We believe it no exaggeration to suggest that of the following incapacities attend the full-fledged hangover.

THE ANATOMY OF MELANCHOLY: PHYSICAL
Bloodshot eyes
Flatulence
Palpitation
Congestion
Headache
Rapid pulse
Heartburn
Restlessness

Dehydration
Hiccups
Diarrhea
Hoarseness
Skin blotches
Disorientation
Hot body surface
Sweating
Diuresis
Hypertension
Dizziness
Tremors
Nausea
Exhaustion

No exaggeration! Some sufferers experience these and even worse effects from having imbibed more alcohol than their systems can handle. Add to the physical results the general mental effects which also accompany a normal hangover, and together the list reads like a masochistic litany of "Adverse Reactions" from the *Physicians' Desk Reference.*

THE ANATOMY OF MELANCHOLY: METAPHYSICAL (MENTAL, SPIRITUAL, PSYCHOLOGICAL)

Anxiety
Guilt
Insomnia
Remorse
Depression
Hypersensitivity
Nervousness

We have made no attempt to list all of the possible reactions of drinking, which include such scary manifestations as temporary color blindness or the inability to hold objects. We speak of normal hangovers and concentrate on major results of normal drinking.

However, be sure of this: anyone suffering from a hangover will, upon careful analysis, realize he or she is experiencing all the physical reactions listed above. Granted, headache and nausea may be playing leading roles at the moment, but exhaustion directs the drama. However, unless you look in a mirror to check for bloodshot eyes, or muster strength enough to use a sphygmomanometer (blood pressure machine—if you own one), such physical manifestations will be playing minor parts at the moment.

As for mental or psychological accompaniment, after a couple hours of restless sleep, insomnia, anxiety, depression, and guilt join the physical chorus. Initially drinking cheered you. After two drinks your spirits soared. But as you continued toward 3:00 a.m. you became circumspective, depressed, even grouchy. After all, alcohol is an anesthetic, a central nervous system depressant, if anything.

Although you are reading this book while sober, remember that "hung over" is different from "drunk." Despite the fact that the British never had a word for it, when an Englishman holds his head and says, "I got exceedingly drunk last evening," he is presently experiencing the current pain and remorse of hangover. He may use other intensifiers such as "blind drunk, beastly drunk or dead drunk" to describe the condition responsible for his after-the-fact suffering.

In a sense, drinking is to hangover as sunbathing is to sunburn. Before you know it, you're overdone. You don't notice the damage right away, but the agony can last for a day or two. (Naturally, the fair-skinned, with ancestry from northern climates, suffer more than Mediterranean types in cases of sunburn or hangover). Yet whether or not you are a careful, circumspect drinker, hangover happens. You didn't think you were in the sun long enough to burn so badly; you couldn't have had nearly enough drinks to make you feel as bad as you do.

A Parade of Fearful Symptoms

Hangover victims experience various symptoms. One may awaken so nauseous that he must throw up, at which point he becomes painfully aware of a throbbing headache.

Another sufferer is experiencing cotton mouth, fuzz throat, THIRST!—a mouth and throat so dry that saliva won't form and he can barely swallow (a condition we labeled "guilty mouth syndrome" in the previous chapter). And how the pulse will race! Normal bedtime pulse rates are about 65-70 beats per minute. But during the early stages of the hangover the rate can double or easily increase 30%. Every possible painful physical and mental effect cries for instant recognition in your exhausted body.

You may find that moaning aloud—an honest display of the pain and mental anguish you feel—helps. Such obvious discomfort may please your bedmate (if you have one), who rarely drinks, and who in fact, is smugly glad you are being punished for the outrageous behavior you reveled in earlier. It could be that your sleeping companion is a source of a good part of the guilt you now feel. However, a cooperative, sympathetic mate can help you along the road to recovery by providing you with the "antidotes" you will be needing-like finding the bathroom!

Part of the nervous anxiety and jitters you are experiencing may be a result of electrolytic imbalance that drinking alcohol can cause—especially potassium and magnesium depletion. As Shakespeare noted, drinking is a "great provoker of urine," and while you were imbibing (especially, if beer), you made frequent trips to the bathroom. When urinating you passed a good deal of magnesium, potassium, and electrolytes in general—a loss which doctors say contributes to a general feeling of uneasiness. Naturally, if you behaved out of character, or acted badly while drinking—you know, told the boss what you really think, got too familiar with shapely Ms. Stuff or hunky Mr. Stud or picked a fight, you are experiencing full-fledged psychological guilt and apprehension along with physical shakiness.

Listed along with other hangover symptoms on the Physical list is one major effect of drinking, notably EXHAUSTION. Drinking can be hard work if you work hard at it. Depending on the situation, you might begin with before dinner drinks, have wine with dinner, then go out to party. If the surroundings are pleasant and the companionship friendly, you might continue drinking until early A.M. Who knows, you may have been standing, walking, talking, coughing, touching, shifting, crying, leaning, patting, slapping, kissing, and the like for as long as six to eight hours—surely an evening's work without drinking!

When you consider all the devastating physical and mental results accruing in hangover, remember that they occur simultaneously with total exhaustion. Your ill and aching body and guilty soul willingly lies abed as long as possible in hopes that time will pass rapidly, and some kind of miraculous healing will happen. Craving sleep, but sleepless, you lie the night long, dreading even the effort of a trip to the bathroom. You wince and writhe in the deepest, darkest depths of the slough of despond.

The Art of Creative Suffering: Inertia is "In-Art"

Dawn finds you supine, languishing in pain like one of Milton's devils on the burning lake. You are in the infelicitous state of INERTIA. Inertia means your very inherent powers of action and motion are dead. You lie inanimate, incapable of physical or mental effort. What a marvelously accurate word, "inertia." How properly descriptive of the condition of hangover! In the original Latin, inertia means "in-art" (as in-capable), the opposite of art. To be inert is to lack art, traits, or skills which make us animate and creative human beings.

Now remember, please, the subtitle of this little volume: The Art of Creative Suffering. Hangover victims must call upon all their power and abilities in an effort to regain humanity. We must summon the imagination to the aid of creative energy (i.e., the Force—remember Luke Skywalker!) in order to feel well again reasonably fast. If we don't consciously recognize our condition and heroically choose to change it, we will certainly suffer all night, all the next day, and perhaps even part of the following night and day, depending on how much alcohol precipitated our current condition and our ability to handle it. It is at this point that the hangover victim must call upon the first two of our Four C's in order to start on the road to complete cure.

THE FOUR C'S

What are the Four C's? Consciousness, Chemicals, Cosmetics and Creativity, all of which lead to the fifth C, Cure.

THE FIRST C: CONSCIOUSNESS

Basically Consciousness means more than merely being aware of your condition due to alcohol. And it means more than simply awakening to your circumstances and realizing your overwhelming need for relief and recuperation. Consciousness means fighting through your physical and mental pain to make a choice to recover as quickly as possible, using all the intellect and energy you can call to your aid.

In one sense, suffering can sharpen your consciousness. Like a long distance runner whose sheer determination carries him through barriers of excruciating pain to a sense of enjoyment and accomplishment in endurance, you too can take pride in choosing to conquer the physical and metaphysical agony that besets you. A proper and lasting cure will result when we engage all Four C's in sequential order. Yes, we must make recovery a ritual. In short, our art will be the re-creation of order in our lives, an order that through art will replace suffering.

THE SECOND C: CHEMICALS

Knowing that no one but yourself has the power to alter the state of hangover, the second of the Four C's must be immediately undertaken upon realizing your condition and consciously choosing to fight back. The experienced drinker chose a long time ago to combat hangover every time he encounters it, so he may automatically bypass the first C, and go directly to the second C—Chemicals—even before he tries to sleep. Drinkers new to the repetitive ravages of hangover must learn to do the same.

Perhaps you've seen the ad on TV where the party-goer returns home late at night, feeling and looking tipsy. His head hurts, his mouth is fuzzy, he moans. However, before he so much as removes his necktie, he heads for the bathroom and plop, plop, fizz, fizz, etc. And since TV commercials only last about a minute, rapid time-lapse shows him going to bed feeling better already. Surely this procedure is a good start for any kind of hangover. However, we recommend Brioschi or Bromo Seltzer before the slower acting Alka Seltzer. All three are satisfactory analgesics, but Brioschi or Bromo Seltzer dissolve more quickly in cold water than does the solid, slow bubbling Alka Seltzer. If you wait for Alka Seltzer to dissolve completely, the advantage of full effervescence is lost. But not so with Brioschi or Bromo Seltzer. However, Alka Seltzer's relatively new Morning Relief has been reported to be quite effective, since it seems to be have been designed specifically for hangover relief.

Over-the-counter "chemicals," such as analgesics (pain relievers) and antacids (alkaline remedies for stomach and intestinal acidity) are generally helpful in normal cases of hangover, and can be very effective taken before bed. The most popular pain reliever today is still aspirin, the "ingredient most doctors recommend for relief of pain," as one analgesic advertiser puts it without ever mentioning the word "aspirin." But aspirin can upset some stomachs, so Bufferin might be a better pain reliever all around. Bufferin has as much aspirin as Bayer, yet it also contains antacids, which help soothe the stomach. And Bufferin enters the bloodstream twice as fast as plain aspirin. The safest nostrum of all is Tylenol because it's composed mostly of Acetaminophen, which won't adversely affect the stomach like aspirin can.

So after drinking, but before bed, try to remember to take a bubbling glass of Brioschi or two tablets of Bufferin. Swallow the Bufferin with a glass of milk for even better stomach-settling results.

If you use aspirin for headache pain before bed you may also want to take two or three teaspoons of Maalox, Riopan Plus, or Mylanta. These antacids will help prevent gastritis, heartburn, and stomach upset from drinking. These soothing liquids are superior to tablets for purposes of hangover since they get to the source of discomfort faster and don't make one nervous through noisy chewing. But the point is to attack head and stomach pain early—before they attack you.

One of the very first symptoms you may face after having drunk considerably is hiccups. The remedy for these involuntary, audible spasms is a teaspoon of granulated sugar. If anything works this should. Hiccups can occur even before you're thinking of leaving the party and are one of the early warning signs of what may be in store for you later.

If you are able, drinking a glass or two of water can only help you before crawling into bed and attempting to sleep. The water won't forestall a parched mouth and throat or the general dehydration taking place due to your discomposed intercellular water balance, but an early start on the condition can lessen "guilty mouth syndrome" the next day.

All these well-intentioned before-bed preparations will help a victim feel both mentally and physically better before sleep, but many can't think about future results at a time when they are exhibiting so much lack of control in general. They flop into bed without caring a whit for pain-prevention, or where they're flinging their clothes.

In any case, the power of drink coupled with exhaustion will almost certainly assure some short rest. Perhaps you'll be lucky enough to sleep until dawn. But more than likely, you'll doze restlessly two to four hours, awaken, lie tossing and turning, while your mind assumes a disproportional guilt for having imbibed so freely and behaved so shamelessly the night before. You may wonder: Do I have to work tomorrow? Is it Saturday? Sunday? Can I ever work again?

You throw the blankets off despite the chill, hold off going to the bathroom, agonize over scenes of what you did or said while "enjoying" yourself, sweat some, and doze into a dream-filled, agitated sleep. Four hours of even this kind of sleep will be fine; five or more hours marvelous. If you didn't treat yourself with chemicals before bed, your physical and metaphysical hangover may be particularly bad by dawn.

Should you confront your hangover on a Saturday or Sunday or a day off, you're in luck. You must stay in bed as long as you can bear the pain lying down, then rise and swallow Bufferin or Tylenol with a half glass of water (the dehydration is insufferable about now) or drink Brioschi, Bromo

Seltzer or Morning Relief if your headache is in equal concert with a nauseous stomach. Should you take aspirin, several spoons of a liquid antacid can't hurt. If you face a workday, you may have to consider calling in sick or pleading that you will be late. You need to buy time to work on your condition.

Although it's morning, your liver has not yet cleared your system of alcoholic intake. As we said earlier, the best it can do is to oxidize about 3/4 of an ounce every hour and a half. So even though you're behaving more docilely, you still are probably legally drunk and should think twice about driving a car. You're not quite ready for Cosmetics yet; more Chemicals may be necessary depending on other side-effects caused by drinking.

Along with headache, a few of the hung-over may find nasal passages congested, stuffiness (along with hoarseness), eyes watery and itchy, and other similar allergic reactions. Some researchers suggest that alcohol produces allergic reactions in certain races of people, especially the Eskimos, the Irish, and American Indians–therefore, the notorious reputations of all three groups as bad-acting and persistent drinkers. Such studies point out that the histamines in wines (as stated, red wines have more than white) and congeners, in whiskies and especially rum (keep in mind the coloring and aging agents in bourbon compared to the relative "purity" of vodkas and gins mentioned earlier) trigger allergic reactions—particularly headaches—in those susceptible. But other medical researchers snigger at such assumptions.

To relieve the physical manifestations of allergic upper-respiratory indications (not asthma) the morning after, one of the many over-the-counter anti-histamines may help.

Of course, you understand that not all the chemicals recommended are to be taken at once or repeated en masse. Part of the duty of the creatively hung-over is to notice what helps from occasion to occasion. Let no hangover pass without instructive results!

THE THIRD C: COSMETICS

Getting off toward complete physical and psychological recovery includes invoking the power of all Four C's, not the least of which is Cosmetics. Of truly great importance to the hangover sufferer is his appearance. The old appearance vs. reality business. Reality (aka: The Puritan Work Ethic!) demands that you reflect physically the ravages of the last night's drinking, pay the piper; that is, look and feel miserable all day long. But Consciousness and Chemicals have started to reverse the process. Oh, you are still sick and exhausted, true, but you refuse to crawl back to bed and suffer. Now you choose to call on the magical restorative powers of Cosmetics, which will help you along to the next stage, where you will experiment with the Creative regenerative recipes of the Cookbook, the most important section of this book.

Before you try to eat, you must engage Cosmetics which means: begin with a complete bath or shower. A shower is best. Adjust the temperature to warm—never a cold shower; your system has been shocked enough. Adjust the flow to a strong volume of water, and soap and rinse your poor body a number of times. Shampoo your hair; emerge squeaky clean. Dry thoroughly, comb, don clean linen and march out of the bathroom and into life as pluckily as Richard Gere (doing his Jerry Lee Lewis imitation) pursues his lady love in the film *Breathless*, just after the television informed him that every cop in Los Angeles was looking for him! Act as if you're the Silver Surfer today.

Without question a drinking male should have an electric razor for A.M. tremors. "Gotcha," the slightest bloody slip with a razor blade can be truly painful and particularly demoralizing in a hung-over condition. And if you are so unfortunate as to break a shoe lace, do nothing for a full 60 seconds. Promise.

Brush your teeth with meticulous care. Slovenliness on a day like this will only highlight to yourself, your family, and anyone who may happen by, all the shortcomings of which you are so painfully aware.

Next it's time for the Visine Vision. Visine or Murine will help get redness out of those bloodshot eyes, a sure elixir for "guilty eyes syndrome" (isn't it surprising how many over-the-counter products advertised regularly on TV are actually manufactured for the single occasion of treating a hangover?). The drops will help ease any irritation resulting from smoke-filled rooms, dust, allergy, and the like. No need to have giveaway red eyes; the tired bagginess from lack of sleep and daydreaming a lot will be reminders enough. And you won't have to avoid mirrors. A light application of, believe it or not, Preparation H around and beneath the eyes will tighten up those pendulous bags. Maybe the "H" also stands for hangover?

Your medicine cabinet ought to hold a small bottle of liquid Vitamin E for any roseola from the night before—those tiny patches of red rash that often appear on the fair-skinned the morning after. Try rubbing a drop of the oil into the "booze blossoms" and see if they aren't faded or almost gone in an hour or so. Cocoa butter is another good skin care product for this kind of redness, and along with Vitamin E oils, E cream, and other healing and blemish covers, is sold at cosmetic counters everywhere. Pride in one's appearance under the most trying conditions is a positive sign and reinforces an opinion of self-worth. Later, you'll feel well enough to work on that little aura of stale alcohol on your breath despite your clean teeth and use of mouth wash. After taking food and taking truly Creative recuperation, you might allow a Turn to dissolve in your mouth.

We shall now move, in our next chapter, to the Fourth, and most important C—that is, Creativity—and through it to the Cure. We have treated the body. Now, via the restorative power of the imagination, we shall treat the major metaphysical effects of the hangover.

MENU

"B&S"

1. One of the major physical requirements for the hangover is sugar. Lots of beverages contain lots of sugar for energy and for the sheer taste of it. So we recommend an ice-cold glass (or two) of regular Pepsi Cola, Coca Cola, Dr. Pepper, or if your taste doesn't run in the cola vein, then Schweppes

Ginger Ale, or Bitter Lemon. There is that mixture of sour/sweet in Schweppes' Bitter Lemon that is nearly sexual in its ability to pleasure one, particularly in a hungover state. The most important detail in administering this cure is that you drink, even quaff, in one fell swoop (or, as James Joyce has it in *Finnegans Wake,* in "one swell poop"; there's that hangover induced malapropism again!). But the quaffing must bring about a loss of breath that you may not have experienced since you were a child. It should leave you breathless and gasping with strange pleasure.

2. If you're not in the mood for re-experiencing child-hood gagging games, then plain old ice tea will do. Lemon-fla-vored Arizona Ice Tea is a favorite with many college students; no single group of people are more consistently experienced in hangover matters than they.

For those of you who would like to transform their hangover pain into a literary experience, there's the T.S. Eliot "J. Alfred Prufrock Cure": Toast and Tea. You're aware that poor old Prufrock had a major problem making up his mind about everything, and his inability to do so may very well be coming from a case of hangover paralysis or, as bad, distrac-tion. Remember Eliot's summary of the fragmented, mod-ern consciousness as "distracted from distraction by distrac-tion." And few phrases could more accurately portray hang-over sensibility.

3. Another favorite college-student recommendation for soups is chili, but it shouldn't be too spicy. It's better when it's a few days old. But if you're too damaged to prepare anything at home, go to your nearest Wendy's, which has the best, most inexpensive chili in America. If you're able to augment your own chili, fry up some ground beef and onions to add bulk. Consume with some of that great Barque Root Beer, also available at Wendy's. Quaff it down till you're breathless!

"F&S"

1. In keeping with our law of simplicity on dark morn-ings (or afternoons, if you've gotten up late), try the great American poet, Wallace Stevens' cure: ice cold celery and

shrimp. He didn't specify this combo as a hangover remedy, but it sure sounds like one. He was known to love his double martinis at his beloved Canoe Club in Hartford, CT. Besides being one the great modern American poets of the 20th Century, he was also a lawyer who worked his way up to become the executive vice president of the Hartford Insurance Company. Also, if you're looking for poetic texts that will take you out of this world with their marvelously Byzantine language, try Stevens' "The Comedian As the Letter C" or "The Man With the Blue Guitar." You have never read anything like them. One theory (mine) about one of Stevens' great early poems "Sunday Morning" is that it's really about a woman trying to deal with her morning-after hangover.

"MP&E"

1. Ground beef—fry in butter with onions and soy sauce and plenty of garlic salt. Get the wide egg noodles (Mueller's are the best), boil them and drench them in butter. Pour the ground burger over the noodles and enjoy. You can tell if it's working because you'll begin to sweat a lot. Chase with Pepsi, Coke, or Dr. Pepper.

2. If you're not in the mood (or shape) to prepare the former, try Stouffer's Beef Burgundy (frozen food); it's easy to fix. The burgundy flavored beef will hit the spot! Italian garlic bread will enhance the taste.

3. If you're in a more creative mood and are going to be cooking up a Sunday dinner anyway, roast pork has everything you need for your hangover: taste, flavor, grease. However, to enhance the pork's innate essence, or, as Aristotle would call its "quiditas" or "whatness," pour a package of onion soup (dry) over it, or a can of onion soup, and drench the roast in garlic salt or powder and add lots of soy sauce. Roast it for as long as it takes (depending on its weight), but leave a little bit of pink at its core. The pork sandwiches from this creation should last you several days, and the delicious gravy will have you looking forward to supper! Consume this roast with cinnamon-flavored apple sauce and roasted potatoes; Schweppes Ginger Ale will add just the right amount of sweet/sourness.

4. For special tastes: There is somewhere in Brooklyn a diner where the seriously hungover used to be able to order Frickadilla, which many claimed was the perfect antidote to any hangover. And here are the ingredients for the great Frickadilla, at least according to my friends Matt and Margaret of Walton, New York: ground pork, ground beef, ground corned beef, and onions—all fried together in bacon grease and then wrapped in bacon and served with greasy home fries. Again, you know it's working when it begins to make you sweat a lot!

"V&S"

1. One of the most effective vegetarian cures is what we call Proustian asparagus. If you're using fresh asparagus, steam it; but don't let it get soggy or limp. After it's done to your taste, lay it on some aluminum foil, sprinkle some parmesan cheese on it and stick it under the broiler till the cheese melts a little. We call this the Proustian cure because no one has written so lovingly about asparagus as the great French novelist, Marcel Proust. In his great novel, *Swann's Way,* he spends an entire page describing the way the sunlight reflects off the asparagus as the main character's aunt prepares the evening meal. In fact, why not read that page as you're preparing your Proustian cure? Soda water might enhance the subtle taste of the asparagus.

2. Connecticut Salad, sometimes known as Polish Salad. Mix some fresh shrimp in with macaroni, mayo, salt and pepper. Or, in place of regular salt, try that old standby, garlic salt. Lemonade will complement the taste of the salad.

"F"

1. A fruit salad of oranges, fresh peaches, apples, and bananas. Use some canned pear juice to hold it all together. The pear juice allows the flavors of the individual fruits to remain distinct.

"D"

1. Peach cobbler or peach pie with plenty of sugar. You might pour some rich cream over it and a dash of cinnamon.

CHAPTER THREE: THE MEDIA

DISTRACTED FROM DISTRACTION BY DISTRACTION

We hope that our first two chapters have supplied your body with satisfactory physical remedies provided by our three C's of Consciousness, Chemicals, and Cosmetics, our unique contribution to this quasi-debilitating condition. We now wish to move you along to our last and most important C, that of Creativity, to complete our Four-Point Program which will enable you to produce your own, unique Fifth C: the Cure (the condition, not the rock group).

We have borrowed a line from T.S. Eliot's *Four Quartets* to embody the essence of the metaphysical hangover sensibility: distracted from distraction by distraction. Since the eyes are the windows of the soul, we shall offer a number of creative suggestions as to what the media (movies and television) has to offer the distracted mental and psychological condition of the typical hangover victim, a condition we have also called the Irwin Corey Syndrome, named after the hero of fragmented consciousness. If the hangover is monumental, you may want to call it the "Richard Cory Syndrome." See the E.A. Robinson poem of the same name.

Thanks to the proliferation of VCRs and DVDs, you can view movies on your own VCR in the comfort of your own home. We'll begin by recommending certain kinds of movies and television shows for their ability to alleviate the discomfort of the metaphysical hangover.

The principal requirement for the most appropriate movie to watch with a hangover is that the movie should contain a Commanding Presence, the same principle that will also apply to the mystery novels in our chapter on Reading. But the choice is broader primarily because great character actors, although able to play many kinds of roles, usually expressed their unique personalities through their roles. For example, any movie with Monty Woolley would be automatically recommended. His peculiar brand of cheerfulness, his sparkling eyes, and white, well-trimmed beard qualify him as a Major Commanding Presence. He was almost always undaunted, optimistic, and most of all, compassionate. But Woolley didn't always portray a compassionate father figure in what many critics consider his greatest role, in *The Man Who Came to Dinner* (1941). Rather he plays an irascible, arrogant writer/radio celebrity who abuses everyone with sarcastic, but always high, wit. His nastiness will delight masochists. One of the more memorable lines from that movie is Woolley's successful threat to clear out the room: "Gentlemen, will you all now leave quietly, or must I ask Miss Cutler to pass among you with a baseball bat?" For a more benign father figure, try him in a 1938 classic, *Young Dr. Kildare.*

Similar traits apply to Charles Coburn, but Coburn's character was usually edged with a certain irascibility. He was benignly cantankerous, but always gave in when a check or a sympathetic shoulder was needed. Don't miss him in the classic *Heaven Can Wait* (1943). We tend to favor movies from the 30's, 40's, and 50's since they featured such strong father figures and didn't seriously attempt to portray reality.

But it's Claude Rains who ranks very high on the hangover scale for a totally different, but equally valid, kind of appeal. To watch him as Hartelius, the composer-conductor, verbally decimate Bette Davis (portraying a pathological liar) in *Deception* (1946) ranks as one of the high marks in the expression of concentrated hatred. It was the way Rains' hair fell over the right side of his large head, the luminous eyes (whose bags had bags, pre-Preparation H), and most of all, the slightly rasping but resonant voice that made Rains the authority figure he was. His arched-browed announcement that Paul Henried was under arrest for murder demonstrated the massive confidence he had in himself, and the hangover victim needs at least the illusion that someone has enough confidence in himself to take charge. The perfect combination, though, would be Monty Woolley's cheerful gregariousness laced with Claude Rains' total confidence. You need to view someone who is both a forgiving father figure and a commanding presence.

Most importantly, however, is that these father figures make moral decisions on clearly defined matters of right and wrong, good and evil. Hangover victims cannot abide moral ambiguity in any form; it drives them crazy. A resolution in which virtue or justice triumphs directly because of the choice of a confident commanding presence will do much to calm the frazzled nerves and wavering decision-making ability of one who overindulged the night before. In other words, the philosophy of "God's in His heaven—all's right with the world!" must prevail even though you may be having serious problems choosing between drinking a Pepsi or a Seven-Up or going to the bathroom now or after the next commercial.

But not all famous actors fit the bill. With Charles Laughton, for example, one must be wary. His facial mannerisms, which he brought to most of his roles, can unwittingly induce "dog's eyes syndrome" (see Chapter Two on this chronic condition), particularly his blinking eyes and twitching cheeks, and get the victim blinking and twitching and making himself quietly hysterical. No wonder his poor wife, Elsa Lancaster, acted the way she did. As Peter Ustinov points out, no actor has ever been able to project the kind of aggressive vulnerability or petulant self-pity that Laughton could embody. It's as if, Ustinov suggests, Laughton's characters sat around waiting for their feelings to be hurt, a feeling that most hangover victims are familiar with. His twitchiest roles were probably *Mutiny on the Bounty* (1935) and *Witness for the Prosecution* (1957).

Laughton is particularly appealing in *Witness for the Prosecution* because he simultaneously portrays a judge totally in charge with a commanding presence, even though he is also obviously a man on the edge, in danger, at times, of flying apart, but holding himself together because of his moral convictions. Indeed, he looks like he has a hangover throughout most of the film and, if you read the biographies, your suspicions are probably correct. Knowing such background information may also help you because you can see a superlative Academy Award winning performance accomplished in spite of a hangover!

The last of these commanding presences is the archetypal Father-Figure of them all, a man who appeared in hundreds of motion pictures: Donald Crisp. Crisp combined many of these qualities into a portrait of the loyal but firm father-figure. He projected a kind of benign Calvinism, pep-talking his recalcitrant sons into ending the strike and going back down into the coal mines for duty's sake. But in *How Green Was My Valley* (1941) he also projected the forgiving father, the monosyllabic great-souled one who, even though he had rarely left his Welsh mining village, had imagination enough to understand his sons' itch to rebel. You're certain that if he were your father he'd give you Holy Hell for your disgraceful behavior of the night before. But you're equally certain that he'd forgive you. And that's what the hangover victim wants more than anything else: forgiveness. Woolley and Coburn would certainly forgive, though perhaps too easily. But with Crisp, you'd feel you earned it. Ma Bell, in her infinite reach-out-and-touch-someone wisdom has supplied the world with Dial-A-Prayer and Dial-A-Joke. Could she not splice together some tapes of Donald Crisp forgiving people and market it as "Dial-A-Pardon?"

Why and how Hollywood lost those characters remains a mystery, but there are simply none around. Can you imagine asking to be forgiven by Marlon Brando, Jack Nicholson, or George Kennedy? I suppose with the disappearance of sin, the onslaught of social scientists and their psycho-babble, and a number of organizations continuing to tell us that nothing is our fault, we don't need mythic father figures to forgive us anymore. There's not only nothing sacred anymore; there's nothing profane anymore either! What to do?

It's the assumption of this book, though, that people still hanker after forgiveness and derive comfort from fictions that present "Prodigal Son" dilemmas. *Tess* (1979), Roman Polanski's brilliant moral film, is about people who can't or won't forgive others and, more importantly, forgive themselves. A highly recommended film for the moderately hungover.

There are, however, a number of females from the same movie generation of the 30's and 40's who could equal and, in some cases, out-forgive even Coburn, Woolley, and Crisp. The four great, archetypal female forgivers are Jane Darwell, Ethel Barrymore, Maria Ouspenkaya, and Sarah Allgood.

Jane Darwell must come first because as Ma Joad in *The Grapes of Wrath* (1940), her forgiveness was massive, immediate and unconditional. With her big watery eyes and a voice that would melt an M&M at ten paces, she instantaneously forgave; no explanation needed nor questions asked. Everyone's forgiven because everybody was drawn into the great Mother Joad of her nourishing LOVE. "Who cares what you've done, I'm your mother and I love you." Jane Darwell is the "Nourishing Mother" incarnate.

With Ethel Barrymore's character, though, it took some time. Highly moral, barely, but finally remembering the memory of passion, she'd relent and in a quavering voice forgive some hedonistic wretch and save him from inevitable suicide or madness. The shaky but softly resonant voice proposed life as tolerable for the sniveling coward and immediately endowed him with the seeds of self-respect. With Barrymore, though, there was sometimes the added dimension of suffering; she was frequently confined in a wheelchair or lay semiconscious in some huge gothic bed. So her special brand of forgiveness seemed doubly earned, carved out of her constant pain and despair. But that's what made it worth the wait. Rumors are she was hungover a lot. Darwell's characters always felt great: well-fed, cheerful, innocent, ready to force feed a platoon. But Barrymore offered forgiveness when she didn't feel like it; she was totally selfless. She earned the right. She could qualify as the movies' first female Christ-figure.

Although the next two female actresses were not major stars like the two above, they each, in their own unique way, contribute to the modern archetype of the Forgiving Mother, but in distinctly different ways. So the hangover victim may have to seek out motion pictures in which they appear.

It's difficult to think of Donald Crisp in *How Green Was My Valley* (1941) without recalling his long-suffering wife, Sarah Allgood, who is so aptly named. Crisp and Allgood were made for one another. But while Crisp projected the Kindly Calvinist, Allgood represented its Irish Catholic counterpart.

The severe dark hair pulled back, lock-jaw moral rigor etched on the face, beneath the ever-worried brow, all restraint disappeared as the sweetest smile this side of Galway Bay suddenly surfaced on her radiant countenance. Unlike Crisp, she was unable to articulate her closely guarded feelings; they were meta-verbal. But she could, as perhaps only Darwell could, physically embody forgiveness, empathy, compassion with tear-filled eyes. The scene in *How Green Was My Valley* in which she lowers her tired head on Crisp's reassuring shoulder as her boys come home from the coal mines, qualifies as the essence of maternal love. Not a dry eye left in the place!

For years, Allgood acted the part of the heart-scalded mother in many of Sean O'Casey's powerful plays which usually included the cruel separation of mothers and sons through poverty, immigration or death. She continued to play the same roles in most of her movies.

The last and perhaps most complex version of the maternal forgiver brings the figure into the 20th century of Freudian psychoanalysis. Maria Ouspenskaya, usually combining the roles of gypsy, witch doctor and wise guide, spent most of her time trying to accomplish two demanding tasks: warn Lon Chaney, Jr. that there were tough times ahead during the next full moon in *The Wolfman* (1940), and imploring him to forgive himself even after he has ripped out Lionel Atwill's throat the night before. Like her Freudian prototype, she kept trying to convince Chaney that it wasn't his fault that he behaved disgracefully. He didn't choose his destiny. It isn't all that difficult to get bitten by werewolves in the mountains of Transylvania. How was he to know?

This updating of the Wolfman story with obvious parallels to *Dr. Jekyll and Mr. Hyde* applies aptly to the hangover victim. Both these stories are about drinking to excess; that is, getting intensely drunk and the disastrous character transformation that then takes place. There's a poem by Edward Rowland Sill that describes the dynamics of the Jekyll/Hyde syndrome:

> *First, the man takes a drink.*
> *Then, the drink takes a drink.*
> *Then the drink takes the man.*

Visualize: Lon Chaney, Jr., gazing at the rounded moon in a valley somewhere north of Bucharest, or Spencer Tracy's face obscenely contorting into a look of ecstatic consternation after quaffing down the libidinous potion. Possibly the reason that Maria Ouspenskaya always looked so washed out was the hassle of having to explain and justify Lon Chaney's periodic behavior to the other gypsies and having to bolt just before things really got, pardon the expression, "hairy."

So if you slipped into your Wolfman or Jekyll-Hyde routine last night at the Elks or the Knights of Columbus Hall, and you feel like Lon Chaney, Jr. looked, watch *The Wolfman* and take courage from those moist Slavic eyes of Maria Ouspenskaya. She's talking to you and she wants to help.

If, however, your nerves are too frayed to watch these particular kinds of movies or you're not in the mood for serious shows of any sort, we recommend a strong dose of a much maligned condition: "Silliness." Lon Chaney's watery eyes or Maria Ouspenskaya's gypsy despair may not help you over your feelings of misery and depression; indeed, they may exacerbate them unnecessarily.

When in doubt, do as your pets do, get silly! Dogs know when and where to act silly and they seem to sense the conditions when their owner needs this kind of activity. The original etymological root of the word "silly" meant "pitiable, happy, and blessed," and various synonyms are "lacking good sense, stupid [especially last night!], frivolous, semiconscious or dazed." Most of these words are virtually synonymous with the usual hangover conditions. If we push the root of the word back to its Indo-European etymon: "sel," we find that it referred to "a person who consoles others by their perpetual good mood." And what could more accurately describe such archetypal "silly people" as Carmen Miranda and Betty Hutton! They, in fact, act as if they were blessed by some visionary experience that convinced them that life is one long, exhilarating dance. We are using the word "silly" in this book, then, in its original etymological and, therefore, deepest sense.

The great linguistic philosopher, Ludwig Wittgenstein (who lost three brothers to suicide) suffered from deep depressions, but he found two rituals that helped him through them. Though he drank little, his symptoms closely resembled those of an acutely hungover person. The first activity that cheered him up was intense and prolonged whistling, a feat that most people with a hangover would find excruciatingly painful (more on the salutary effects of whistling in the next chapter). It is rumored that he could whistle the entire *Mendelssohn Violin Concerto* note-perfect and from memory. His other custom was to go to the movies and sit in the front row so as to get as far into the movies of either Carmen Miranda or Betty Hutton as was humanly possible. Thank heavens the VCR dub has since entered our lives! He venerated these women because their "High Silliness" presented a world brimming with cheerful optimism, a declared fiction, a slam-dance response to his constant depression. For the hangover victim, Carmen Miranda represents a dancing tree, a dance of nature. In fact, the Latin root of her name literally means "song" (carmen) of "astonishment or wonder" (miranda). And anyone who has seen her in those lush movies of the 40's and 50's are left in a condition of wonder at this exotic bird-woman singing lyrics no one understands or needs to. See her in *Nancy Goes to Rio* (1950).

In *The Greatest Show on Earth* (1952), Betty Hutton dances on a galloping horse as though she had grown out of it, swinging on a trapeze like some prehistoric "Lucy" reenacting the "Fall." Outside of the obvious silliness of these two fey creatures, their amoral celebration of Being obliterates the need for forgiveness or any serious consideration of guilt. They are what life is all about: the Dance.

The only male that comes anywhere near the magnetic pull of Miranda or Hutton is the 20th century's sweetest, best-natured, and most understanding teenager, Sabu the Elephant Boy, who starred in a number of vivid technicolor movies during the 40's and 50's in which he guided stuffy Englishmen into the dark, liberating mysteries of the East. He is the male counterpart of Carmen Miranda, since he also appears to derive his power from nature. His most famous picture is the unforgettable *Thief of Baghdad* (1940). And like Hutton and her horse, he appears in most films as an extension of whatever elephant he's riding at the time. He's not as silly as the two women but comes off as an Indo-European version of Shakespeare's Puck from *Mid-Summer Night's Dream*.

Besides these three classic archetypal silly people, other minor movie characters serve the same function, but to a lesser degree. Though they were not necessarily the stars of the movies in which they appeared, their personalities were so compelling that they invariably stole scenes even though their dialogue was vapid and their actions trite. Like Barry Fitzgerald, they, too, could steal scenes from dogs and children. Perhaps the most notable character, besides Fitzgerald himself, was Billie Burke who played Glenda, the Good Witch of the North in *The Wizard of Oz*. In fact, she played a version of that role in just about every movie she ever made. She fluttered and chirped non-stop. And the counterpoint of her high-pitched twitter coupled with the basso profundo of Eugene Pallette was immediately hilarious regardless of what they were discussing. To see them together; she, petite and fairy-like and he, with three chins and weighing in at about 330, was a visual joke. But whatever scene she appeared in, she would immediately trivialize the point of discussion. She simply could not be serious about anything and saw no reason to.

The same trivializing scene stealing was also the province of the wonderfully comic Una O'Connor, a mousey, permanently aproned servant who was forever fretting over her master or mistress's health, warmth, or mood. She was the Irish servant *par excellence* who, as soon as her English masters left the room, verbally vilified them for their bloodless boredom and empty lives. Though O'Connor was genuinely silly, her servant roles almost always had a political edge to them especially in such films as *Witness for the Prosecution* (1957). She laced her silliness with occasional venom and could roar like a lion or purr like a kitten when the situation demanded. Don't miss her in *The Bride of Frankenstein* (1935).

For an actress who was never not silly and who added a dimension of empty frivolity to most of her roles, no one could approach Spring Byington. She projected a squeaky cleanness that made everybody else in the room appear innately depraved. Her concerns were always social but on the most banal level. She played the social chairwoman of cultural clubs that actually called themselves The Culture Club, usually a group of antiseptic elders, whose collective presence was so dull it was interesting. Spring Byington's smile, though, and her breathless enthusiasm about everything, will sweep away most hangover gloom at least temporarily. The most damaged hangover victim will find solace in either Billie Burke's fairy freshness, Una O'Connor's mousey petulance, or Spring Byington's good-natured froth.

Don't think for a moment though, that there weren't any silly men. There were plenty. The father of them all was undoubtedly the famous character actor of dozens of technicolor MGM 50's films, S.Z. (Cuddles) Sakall. He was an immensely compelling grandfather archetype, and there would be no question of being forgiven by "Cuddles." The most obvious reason he would forgive you is that he never seemed to understand what anybody was talking about; nothing seemed to register: "Vat you mean you 'dropped trow' at party? I no understand." But his principal function was never saying anything very intelligible; he was the greatest mumbler in Hollywood history. And when he did say something, it rarely made any sense. His routine was to roll his kindly blue eyes, shake his Jell-o-like jowls and proclaim his ignorance of what was going on. He, like Spring Byington, was too busy fussing over inane details to hear, much less comprehend, what was going on around him. Don't miss him in top form with Judy Garland and Van Johnson in *In the Good Old Summertime* (1949). He was, in T.S. Eliot's words, distracted from distraction by distraction, a phrase that as accurately as we know describes the metaphysical hangover. For the illusion of a little warm cuddling and Grandfatherly concern, "Cuddles" Sakall is your man.

The king, though, of sophisticated bumpkins must be the Dr. Watson of the *Sherlock Holmes* films starring Basil Rathbone. More will be said about these films, though, toward the end of this chapter. How Nigel Bruce's Dr. Watson ever passed his medical boards remains a permanent mystery. Or how he managed to moderate his massive pull towards permanent silliness long enough to examine a murder victim with any kind of thoroughness defies the imagination. Like a victim of Korsakoff's Syndrome, Nigel Bruce immediately forgot what he and Holmes had just discussed. His figure, though, still exerts a strong attraction for hangover victims possibly because the combination of silliness and distraction tranquilizes their fractured mental processes. Watson is also relentlessly cheerful and agrees with anything that is said. His dialogue was one long series of "Why, yes, of course, Holmes!" A habit, by the way, that might come in handy at work the next day. So if the night before was a rough one, do your Nigel Bruce routine and you may avoid trouble. Bruce created the illusion of actually accomplishing some task when in reality he was incapable of performing the simplest assignment. So learn well from such a consummate faker. Bruce was known in real life as a two-fisted drinker of the first order.

These characters not only comfort the suffering by their presence, they also teach you practical ways of behavior on hangover days, ways that will enable you to go to work and get some things done but look as though you're accomplishing much more.

There are other memorable minor character actors who projected silliness in one permanent role and, usually, via a particular part of their anatomy. Who could forget the way Billie De Wolfe, Mischa Auer, or Leon Errol used their eyes as the focal point of their routine. Mischa Auer's eyes (like a dog's eyes) could run through twenty to thirty emotions a minute. And that was when he was calm! Unlike the random, autonomic brow movements of dogs, his eyes were instruments of high art alternating grace notes with glissandi that suggested the most precious distinctions between, say, bitchiness and petulance, flirtation and seduction. He practically steals the show with a performance boarding on High Camp (before there was a name for it) in *You Can't Take It With You* (1938), and he is up against very stiff competition with such Commanding Presences as Edward Arnold, Lionel Barrymore, the voice of Spring, Spring Byington, the archetypal "Clean Old Man" Harry Davenport, and the meekest of the meek, Donald Meek himself (though he could be *very* bitchy).

Billie De Wolfe, though, used his popping eyes in an aggressively dainty way. But if you stretch your memory a long way back, you'll recall the ferret-like squint of the permanently cantankerous Leon Errol, a character, by the way, as crudely direct as De Wolfe was cleverly urbane. Leon Errol's ever-present squint-scowl registered better than few in movie history, a perpetual exasperation with everything: children, flowers, refrigerators and especially vampy women. De Wolfe's loony eye popping could serve as an antidote to Errol's arched-eyed disapproval and vice versa. Though they may be hard to locate, see Errol's sputtering depiction of Lord Epping in the *Mexican Spitfire* series of the 40's. Their sets are frighteningly empty.

As far as contemporary eyes go, few are as riveting as Don Knotts in both the *Andy Griffith Show* and his forays into the Disney films. He qualifies as a prime example of eye popping at its most neurotic. Knotts' marvelously facile eyes possess both the dexterity of De Wolfe and the sensitivity of Auer, but they express a deeper, almost existential panic that the earlier models lacked. They can project, in the middle of some slapstick routine, genuine terror and guilt, resembling the eyes of some hangover victims the morning after as they are desperately trying to listen to and remember their supervisor's instructions.

So, depending on the severity of the hangover, pay attention to the eyes of these unique performers who are masters of distraction.

If, for some reason, you can't focus on human behavior and the funniest faces appear twisted with pain, à la Ingmar Bergman, try concentrating on animals but only under very specific conditions. Avoid at all costs documentaries on animals. Though they are extremely educational, the reality of how animals actually behave according to natural laws is not the kind of information one needs with a hangover. The "morning after" is not the time to learn about our part in the natural cycles. You simply cannot endure an entire hour on the undulating termite mother and all the silent horror that goes into protecting her from the billion ants that are marching inexorably toward her mud castle on any given summer afternoon.

Hungover people can, however, handle animals much more comfortably when they behave like silly or super-wise human beings. Of course, the king of Jungle Silliness is the beloved Cheetah of the *Tarzan* movies. Indeed, he usually put in better performances than either Tarzan or Jane. Cheetah's facial expressions (like dog's eyes!) may pull you into what people project (the old "pathetic fallacy" of John Ruskin) as human emotions: joy, anger, lechery, melancholy, blankness, etc.—all in seven seconds! Be careful, though, of shows featuring Lassie especially the ones from the 40's with Roddy McDowall and Donald Crisp. They are handsomely rendered films but are heart-breaking, and if you tend to burst into tears during a hangover, you'd best avoid their aching sadness. Certainly the television series *Lassie* will fill the bill since they are highly formulaic and never become oppressively bleak.

For the healthiest form of animal watching, try re-runs of *Flipper.* The sunshine, the water, and the humor of Flipper himself will make you feel better. Luke Halpin, the TV "Boy on a Dolphin" ranks as the cleanest teenager on the tube and also qualifies as the Orphic interpreter of what Flipper is trying to express. He's the aquatic version of Sabu the Elephant Boy, a dispenser of natural wisdom, just what a dark day could use.

Of course, Walt Disney built an empire on his belief that animals (humanized always, however) are the last bastions of wisdom and common sense in an age where self destruction masquerades as self help. Only animals seem to have much hope to offer mankind and, because your nerves on hangover days are super-sensitive, you tend to read significance into their facial expressions and body movements. Disney always superimposed the human upon the animal so that when you observe monkeys, you unconsciously view them as hairy babies combining fluent muscular coordination with devastating wit. And since Americans are the last romantics, we are prepared to believe some creature from a vernal wood (monkeys, dogs, chipmunks) more readily than the accumulated wisdom of the sages. Well, who knows? Monkeys never have hangovers, or do they? Once more, the Chinese proverb: "Life is a drunken monkey."

There may be, however, some of you who are uncomfortable with and unable to focus on any of these characters whether they be Commanding Presences, Forgiving Earth Mothers, or Major Embodiments of Holy Silliness. And animals may turn you off since you don't accept the American concept of animal wisdom or they simply make your skin crawl. What we propose for those of you who can't connect on a human or animal level is a geographical cure; that is, a focus on place. There are selected movies and television shows where place or settings are as compelling as the characters. These places should be soothing, safe, and most importantly, *cozy*. They should be warm, neat, and preferably small, a place where you can hide away in your imagination from the conflicts of everyday life. Nothing embodies this sort of redemptive coziness so brilliantly as the inviting cottages, babbling brooks, and protective mountain mothers of Thomas Kinkade, self-proclaimed "painter of light." His alluring scenes of glowing windows have made him America's wealthiest landscapist, an industry unto himself, complete with mall outlets.

Remember as a child, how inviting Jerry's little mousehouse seemed in the Tom and Jerry cartoons, especially Jerry's little match-box bed? We ache for Tarzan's tree-house once Jane domesticates it. And even though you may want to avoid the complicated plots of most Tarzan films, merely viewing the natural coziness of the tree lodge could bring some relief from the metaphysical shudder that hangovers can cause. That morning vulnerability could be substantially reduced along with the sense of being locked inside your skin (dermatological claustrophobia) by taking refuge inside the Tarzan Bunker with a spectacular view of the forest cathedral. Of course, it's another regenerated Eden, the same one that shows up in *Swiss Family Robinson* (1960), after the kids start arriving.

For cozy settings from television and film, there is the perfect house of Dagwood Bumstead (minus the revolting dog!),

Lucy and Desi's quaint living room, and the kitchen of the Nelson family where Ozzie plays Goofy Dad.

However, the archetypal Cozy home has to be the digs of Sherlock Holmes himself at 221 B Baker Street in London. These rooms are the most comfortable lodgings in cinema history. The domesticated Holmes with the ever-present pipe, smoking jacket, and slippers, the fire that Mrs. Hudson always keeps burning and Dr. Watson (Nigel Bruce) muttering harmlessly, become "Eden in the City," protected from, but adjacent to, the heart of urban life just outside the door. It's where folks with hangovers would love to hang out; it's the Great Good Place.

We conclude this chapter, as we shall with our chapter on reading, with a listing of our twenty most highly-recommended movies and TV shows to watch with a hangover, and a short justification for our choice. We have tried to combine characters, plots, and settings to give you the best chance of displacing, at least for a while, the prevailing sense of doom that a hangover can cause. Of course, the films listed above during our discussion of special characters and settings are also included in our recommendations.

SPECIAL CATEGORY

Believe it or not, there are two films with the word in the titles. *The Big Hangover* (1950) features Liz Taylor, Van Johnson, Leon Ames and a talking dog. We've not been able to view it and critics are divided on its artistic merits, but it sounds as though it could have been written with a hangover. The other, *Hangover Square* (1945) was Laird Cregar's last film. He portrays a mad, murderous composer. Three walks around this fictional London square was supposed to cure hangovers—thus the name.

1. *The Red Shoes* (1948). We believe this is possibly the best film ever made for complete relief from the hangover. It has everything: great music, settings in London, Paris and Monte Carlo plus the magnificent jealousy of Anton Walbrook as the elegant Lermontov. It's serious Camp.

2. *Random Harvest* (1942). One of the great mothers of all hangover victims, Greer Garson and an actor who could belch elegantly, Ronald Coleman, who is really suffering from a prolonged booze blackout and is nursed back to consciousness by Dame Greer.

3. *Doctor Zhivago* (1965). Domestic Russian settings before the revolution. One of the great losses of the revolution was their inviting settings. Great music, Julie Christie's unspeakable beauty and Omar Sharif's bloodshot eyes will make you grateful for the post-revolutionary invention of Visine.

4. *The Third Man* (1949). A work that is possibly the longest sustained mood of mystery in movie history, thanks to its vivid black and white scenes and the haunting gypsy zither of Anton Karas. Vienna trashed after WWII and all that goes with it. Orson Welles is charmingly evil, a real Satanic performance.

5. *Dr. Jekyll and Mr. Hyde* (1941). The Spencer Tracy-Ingrid Bergman version. Quaint London settings and one of Tracy's best performances. His transformation scenes after quaffing the potion may remind you of yours the night before after the third Stinger.

6. *It's a Wonderful Life* (1946). If your hangover guilt is so bad that you're thinking of leaping off a bridge, see how an angel saves James Stewart from a similar fate.

7. *The Bank Dick* (1940). Classic W.C. Fields (probably hungover) and his role as a bank guard. There is a sadistic hangover scene in this film in which Fields deliberately tries to make a very hung-over Franklin Pangborn even sicker by suggesting nauseating food remedies. It's Fields at his cruelest. See the recipe for "The W.C. Fields Sadistic Hangover Cure."

8. *Amarcord* (1974). Fellini's non-surreal memoir of his youth and full of gentle warmth and vivid characters. Very soothing Italian settings with goofy teenaged boys jerking off together in an old car.

9. *Excalibur* (1981). The King Arthur Grail myth filmed in spectacular Irish settings, forest chapels, and laced with Wagner's music throughout. Soothing medieval magic will calm jangled nerves.

10. *The Day the Earth Stood Still* (1951). A classic black and white sci-fi of a visitor from outer space who warns us to be nice to one another, or else. Clean 50's Washington, D.C. settings and a space ship on the White House lawn with Patricia Neal supplying lots of forgiveness and the last boarding house in America.

11. *Last Year at Marienbad* (1962). A surreal film so cryptic that a hangover sensibility could help explicate it. But it is visually dazzling and Delphine Seyrig is hauntingly beautiful. It may actually be about someone remembering a blackout and what really happened.

12. *Footloose* (1984). Kevin Bacon reintroduces the Dionysian Dance back into a permanently Calvinized Colorado community and gets into a lot of trouble. Bacon takes over where Carmen Miranda left off in 1955 without pineapples on his head.

13. *Diva* (1982). Perhaps the smoothest film ever made. It has music, mystery, young love and French sophistication made palatable even for us dumb Americans. The sustained musical mood will keep hangover gloom at arms' length.

14. *La Cage aux Folles* (1978). You will laugh out loud in spite of your splitting headache! Here are the French who invented High Silliness at their best with warm, soothing French Riviera settings.

15. *Blow Up* (1967). The great Italian director, Antonioni, plays around with phenomenological possibilities. You're never sure what really happened and this film seems to be just the right one for those suffering from "guilty eyes syndrome." It's like trying to piece things together the day after. It takes place in London, but it could be Paris. What difference does it make?

16. *Rose Marie* (1936). The beauty, charm and shining face of Jeanette MacDonald will cauterize most hangover dejection, especially when she and Nelson Eddy sing the "Indian Love Call." Scenes of Canadian Rockies will help alleviate any residual dermatological claustrophobia.

17. *Sons of the Desert* (1933). Any of the Laurel and Hardy films will help with hangover depression, but this is probably their funniest full-length film. They are lodge brothers at a

convention misbehaving badly. For the single funniest "getting drunk" scene in film history, see them quaffing it down in *The Devil's Brother* (1933). They're emptying out wine barrels and can't find any place to pour it, so they drink it with predictable results. Guaranteed to make you laugh out loud! You could even have "an accident"!

18. *The Thing* (1951). The dialogue is really funny and the Arctic Quonset Huts are strangely comforting. Don't go near the 1982 remake because the goo-creatures will make your skin crawl and cause serious trauma for the hypersensitive hungover victim.

19. *Seven Beauties* (1976). A story of an Italian survivor in a Nazi concentration camp. If he can survive, certainly you can with your minor discomfort. Some of the scenes are grotesquely hilarious.

20. *That's Entertainment Pts. I and II* (1974 and 1976). Since our project is to get you as close to Dance as possible, psychologically that is, these scenes from classic musicals of MGM fit the bill. All the giants are there: Astaire, Gene Kelly, Eleanor Powell, Garland, Bing Crosby, etc. to demonstrate that it is possible to recreate an age of innocence and believe in it for awhile.

TELEVISION: THE MACHINE IN THE GARDEN

VCRs and DVDs are ideal instruments with which to treat your hangover but careful selection of television programs, especially re-runs, is recommended. Be especially cautious when turning on the TV and being exposed to whatever may pop up. A regularly hungover associate claimed that on several occasions, he had fastened onto one of those brutal nature programs on the eternally recurring destiny of African Wildebeests on their spectacularly depressing yearly migrations that have been going on for eons. They cross the same river in the same impossible place and lose thousands of the group. The ones that don't get swept away become prime targets for the lions that are waiting silently (and have been forever) twenty miles across the plains. You don't need the vividly brutal lives of wildebeests today.

Also to be avoided are re-runs of chaotic serials such as *Dobie Gillis* and, worst of all, *Gilligan's Island*. Anarchy reigns on these adolescent shows. Nobody seems in charge so you are missing a reassuring Commanding Presence. There is also no domestic center from which some kind of order emerges. An unfocused gang of teenagers at a soda fountain is simply too overloaded with emotional possibilities. And the peculiar brand of 50's Puritanism, combined with the constant sexual connotations that repression stimulates, will drive an already overwrought hangover consciousness beyond distraction.

Much safer would be the peace engendered by the Three Kings of domestic tranquility: Ozzie Nelson, Ward Cleaver, and Robert Young. The last refuge for everybody is the family show. A more mature and presumably widowed Robert Young reappears years later as *Marcus Welby, M.D.*, but serves the same function as a wise, fatherly guide always in charge. The settings in all of these family shows, in spite of the spotless Cleaver household, can serve as tranquil refuges of coziness.

Beyond domestic safety, family security, and the illusion of belonging, the most highly recommended commanding presence would certainly be Perry Mason. If LA were swept away by THE earthquake, Mason would maintain total control and casually send Paul out to see what's left. Mason's law office is so 50's that it could appeal to those of you who are consoled by banal emptiness. Mason is the master of logic and ratiocination, a condition that is so foreign to you in your hungover state that it will seem as though he is performing major miracles before your very eyes. Large doses of awe usually help.

For best results, and guaranteed to make you laugh no matter how wrecked you may feel the day after, is the ever-present *I Love Lucy*. She never fails because her humor is somehow plugged into a kind of healing madness, a crazy wisdom that could make you forget just about anything. The Arnez living room, a domesticated version of Perry Mason's bland office, will engender a kind of comic serenity. And when you have settings that can do this, you know you are in the presence of genius.

If you are selective, some home improvement shows may

help if the tasks they are working on are not too complicated. As long as they are doing something that you, in good shape, could see yourself doing, like fixing a wooden gate or painting a room, they're O.K. But beware of major remodeling projects, highly complex activities such as adding a room to the house or putting in a swimming pool and the kind of re-routing of plumbing demanded by such a project. *Turn off* the TV.

Also, cooking shows are acceptable if the projects are simple. But if much complicated cutting away meat from the bone, especially veal, is featured or exotic meats such as brains or inner organs like kidneys or gullets are thrown about, it would be best to switch channels. Vegetables and fruits are, as in real life, soothing and watching them assume other forms may appeal to your fractured creative impulses. Also, foreign cooks who speak broken English could drive you crazy because in your condition you won't be able to understand much of what is being said. However, if you need order, nothing fits the bill like *Iron Chef*. The best, though, is the wonderful chef of French cooking, Julia Child. She's articulate and, although she seems distracted, she really isn't. She can also shift from scenes of enormous chaos to creating absolute and delicious order within an hour's time, a kind of culinary objective correlative of what our book is trying to accomplish in the disordered "kitchen" of your psyche. Her accompanying remarks are always sophisticated and witty. If she were an actress, she would certainly qualify as a Forgiving Mother Figure *par excellence,* feeding her guilt-laden children.

As for early morning news shows, we recommend warm and gentle personalities; that is, human beings who exude confidence and mental health. Our favorites include Harry Smith, whose compassion, gentle nature and ability to laugh at himself may comfort the hungover, and Al Roker, the perfect weatherman for dark mornings, who seems to get a kick out of everything, even a hangover. Avoid at all costs weathermen/women who clown around while seeming to assume guilt for the coming ice storm. They relish their status as meteorological sin-eaters and professional breast beaters. Not today, please!

Matt Lauer strikes just the right balance between an overly unctuous milksop and the flinty pugnacity of long-gone Bryant Gumbel. Whatever became of the single most comforting weatherman in TV history, Mark McEwen? Seek out the Three Graces who appear with Harry Smith, whose cumulative radiance will brighten the shakiest morning. Beware, though, of Paula Zahn, whose re-emergence on CNN shows a much more aggressive figure. She has become very pushy, interrupting her guests repeatedly. Her unblinking stare—those Germanic blue-azure eyes—can generate a Medusa-like paralysis not to be trifled with.

As for major network television programs, we highly recommend re-runs of *Twin Peaks*, principally for its settings of Edenic tranquility and woody coziness. It is also hilariously funny in a very dry way and may be the first consistent form of subtlety to appear on American television. If, however, you are too damaged to appreciate its sophisticated humor, you can take it all literally and treat it as a serious crime show with one of the strangest Commanding Presences ever created in Kyle MacLachlan's FBI techno-nerd. The music is ideal for a hangover because it possesses an eclecticism that could appeal to virtually any level of consciousness from the hypersensitive to the nearly comatose.

Of afternoon and late-night talk shows, be careful with Jerry Springer because the poor souls represented are never going to be anything else in their lives but poor souls. And that thought is too unbearably dreadful for the hungover. Letterman and Conan are perfect for the condition because their humor is consistently off-center and, therefore, close to true hungover sensibility. Both highlight the essential absurdity of life, but with humor and self deprecation. As good is *Oprah!* Though she presents some dark, depressing lives, she always leaves room for optimism. Things can always get better with HELP. And that's what chronic hangover sufferers most need to hear.

We shall now move on to a consideration of what one may, can, should and should not read on the morning after in our progressive journey through the possibilities of our fourth and your fifth C: Creativity and Cure.

Remember that our creative projects will, if used, help you create your own cure for your particular hangover because in such a condition, your sole refuge, after applying the requisite Chemicals, Cosmetics, and Consciousness, is your own unique imagination and its infinite capabilities.

MENU

"B&S"

1. A writer friend of ours swears by the ameliorating effects of, believe it or not, Ovaltine; but he says that you must drink it warm. Remember Ovaltine's early motto that you may have heard on the radio: "Drink Ovaltine at night and wake up gay the next morning!" My, how language has changed!

2. Ice-cold milk, either regular or chocolate. If you're in the mood for high calorie milk, try the Nesquik in either the chocolate or very-vanilla bottled form. They're very rich and very sweet! If you must have your morning coffee, make it decaf. Avoid at all costs regular coffee because what you will create is an extremely alert hungover person who will moan and complain twice as much.

3. Bill Gorton, a character in Hemingway's great novel, *The Sun Also Rises,* recommends goat's milk as a Spanish peasant remedy for hangover. The novel is full of much drinking and most of the characters are very hungover. One waggish literary critic attributes Hemingway's revolutionary prose style to the hungover condition in which he almost always wrote. While virtually no writer worth his salt would write while drunk or stoned, many of them—at least the modern American and British ones—wrote with hangovers: Faulkner, Cheever, Carver, Steinbeck, Thomas Wolfe, Sinclair Lewis, Robert Lowell, E.A. Robinson, Evelyn Waugh, Henry Green, Graham Greene, Joyce and many others.

4. The most effective healing soup is vegetable beef. Fry up some ground beef and onions to add bulk to the soup; add wide noodles with plenty of butter. A dash of soy sauce and garlic salt will intensify the flavor.

"MP&E"

1. If you're fortunate enough to live near a Jewish deli-catessen, you'll be able to procure the classic Yiddish Hangover Cure: a hot corned beef or pastrami sandwich with yellow mustard and Kosher pickles. Better yet, the same sandwiches, but instead of rye bread, use latkas—potato pancakes. Tears of pleasure and gratitude will appear involuntarily. Let them flow. You might play recordings of genuine Gypsy music or Polish/Russian folk dances while reveling in your sandwiches. Or better yet, watch any old movie with cozy Gypsy settings in the background: darling little Gypsy horsecart mobile homes with Transylvanian forests and mountains in the back-ground. The recent *Van Helsing* movie sets are perfect, but beware the violence that's going on in the town square from the castrating virgin bitch goddess zombies wreaking havoc all over the place.

2. Another hangover favorite is a classic Austrian/Hungarian HO cure: open-faced ground beef sandwich. Take half a hamburger bun and spread a goodly amount of ground beef on it; broil it with cheese on top (Swiss or yellow ched-dar). A tomato on top will add vitamins. Cook them medium rare so that some of the blood soaks into the bun. Sop it up!

3. Chicken breasts baked in mushroom soup. Pour over biscuits. Add butter. Any kind of barbecue, but especially Brooks' Barbecue Sauce of Oneonta, New York. It's the best. Brooks' also makes sauce for ribs—either pork or beef. If you can't get it near your home, you can send for it at the follow-ing address: Brooks' House of Bar-B-Q's, East End, Oneonta, NY 13820 or visit their website at www.brooksbbq.com.

"F&S"

1. Some friends from Annapolis, MD, swear by what they call the Seafood Cure: it is a version of one of the great American delicacies: Maryland Crabcakes. There is also a won-derfully unique memoir by that marvelous African-American novelist and short-story writer, James Alan McPherson, actual-ly called *Crabcakes*. It's his favorite food. Mine, too! It's a uniquely serene book, and if you're looking for a calming

memoir, you can't go wrong with this spiritually rewarding masterpiece. McPherson is one of *the* great American short story writers.

2. If you're into something a bit simpler, tuna fish is your answer. Every time I open a can of tuna fish, I am amazed that it isn't as expensive as the best caviar; it tastes like such a delicacy, especially the white, albacore kind. Consuming it right out of the can doesn't detract one bit from its pleasure-giving. I'm sure the only reason that tuna fish isn't as expensive as the finest caviar is that there are so damn many tuna fish—billions of them—all over the place. But even in a damaged HO state, one can still open a can, dump it in a dish and mix it up with mayo or, better yet, Miracle Whip, sliced onions, a little sweet pickle juice. Eat it out of the bowl or make a tuna fish sandwich with sweet pickles. Schweppes Ginger Ale makes a fine accompanying beverage. But if you're drinking Pepsi or Coke, add a handful of Fritos. Get ready for a memory rush from when you were eight years old!

"V&S"

1. A friend of mine from Hungary suggests an old remedy from the Jewish section of Budapest. It's called the Vinegar Cure. Simply slice up some cucumbers and onions, and drench them in vinegar. Add plenty of pepper. You'll gasp!

2. Also the great pianist, Alexander Toradze, offers a cure from his home country of Georgia: slice up some regular and red cabbage, with onions, cucumbers, celery, and peas and soak in vinegar. Add lots of pepper.

"F&D"

1. Ice cold plums. To add a bit of American literary history, try reading the early poems of one of America's greatest poets, William Carlos Williams—the great celebrator of the body and its available pleasures in any and all modes. Williams was also a practicing pediatrician for many years in Rutherford, New Jersey. He wrote a small masterpiece titled "This is just to say" and it's a poem about eating (and really enjoying) ice-cold plums. Before it was a poem, it was a note

he wrote his wife apologizing for eating the plums that she was keeping in the refrigerator for breakfast the next morning. Williams simple rearranged the note into 3 stanzas, thus creating a poem out of a casual note. Williams' poems—especially the early ones—would be perfectly appropriate to read on hangover mornings. They celebrate the fact that we're alive, regardless of what condition we may be in.

There is a scene in that masterpiece movie, *American Beauty,* in which the young dope peddler (who is routinely beaten by his repressed homosexual Marine colonel father) shows the protagonist's daughter a 10-minute film of a plastic bag being blown about by the wind in his driveway; he recognizes the profound beauty of that image. Well, the appreciation of the sublimity of the common experience is William Carlos Williams' specialty. But he does it with fruit (peaches, plums, oranges) and huge brown bags run over by trucks, rising again in all their resurrected quotidian glory.

"D"

1. Keep on hand of bunch of red seedless grapes and some Jell-O in those little pre-prepared cups. (Green seedless grapes will do just as well.) Combine two or three of the Jell-O cups in a bowl and mix in the grapes. Cherry or strawberry Jell-O go well with grapes. Canned peaches in Jell-O can be just as delicious as grapes; there's just something so comforting about peaches. Even J. Alfred Prufrock might enjoy them! Yes, Prufrock, in one of your rare unguarded moments, go ahead and Eat a Peach! And let the juice run down your chin, too!

CHAPTER FOUR: FROM MUSE-SICK TO MUSIC

If you recall, we began our book with a listings of things not to do with a hangover such as drinking any form of alcohol, visiting zoos, calling up your fellow celebrants from the night before and asking them what you did, etc. So to begin our chapter on Music, we'd like to repeat two earlier taboos and add two more right off the bat:

—*Stay away from Mexican and Central and South American music* in most forms. As we stated earlier, the excessive busyness of both the rhythmic patterns and elaborate melodic developments will be impossible to follow. Jumpy music will make you even jumpier, and this is definitely not the time for Mexican hat dances. We do have an exception listed in a later section of this chapter.

—*Avoid at all costs High School Band Concerts* and especially High School Band *Contests.* Groups of endlessly energetic adolescents generate a kind of manic tension that is unique. Teen hysteria is impossible to write about with much accuracy, and most authors fall into nostalgic sentimentalism. However, you know it when you are surrounded by it. Band concerts, along with basketball games and, oddly enough, wrestling matches, where audiences frequently "lose it" in enclosed areas could really drive you beyond endurance. Outdoor band concerts or sports events held in the open enable teen manic hysteria to release itself, mercifully, into the atmosphere.

—*Avoid Chinese and Japanese operas* for obvious reasons.

—*Avoid concerts of Scottish bagpipes* because, as in the case of Mexican music, your overwrought aural capacity will simply not be able to hone in on one or two themes. Trying to find *a* theme and follow its development within the clutter of bagpipe music is a thankless task in the best of mental states.

However, if you want to flirt with a form of non-surgical lobotomy, and are feeling deeply masochistic, dare to listen to *anything* by Spike Jones and his City Slickers. Only the more mature readers will remember him. Today may not be the best day to confront Ishcabibel or Sir Frederick Gas.

MUSICAL EXORCISM: A CONTINUING "SPIRITUAL" BATTLE

The word "music" comes from the same etymological root as the words "muses," "Museum," "amusement," and so on. And, as most of you probably know, the "Muses" are those spirits that inspire artists. On hangover mornings, you could easily spell the word "muse-sick" since your muses are undoubtedly not well. The point is that the "distilled spirits" with which you were involved the night before will now have to do battle with the actual, unabstracted "spirits" in their musical form—from muse-sick to music, as it were. Our major requirement for the kind of music to begin with is that it be in some way *compelling*.

Our rationale for choosing such a word is consistent with the metaphor of the "spiritual" battle that you must wage the morning after. In the Roman Catholic manual of rituals, *The Racolta,* the key word used in the ceremony of Exorcism is "compel." The exorcist keeps repeating the word, if you recall from that great movie, *The Exorcist,* "We compel you to leave the body of so and so …." In like manner, we offer three recommendations for specific pieces of music which could immediately exorcise the demonic spirits of the night before by their compelling qualities. Keep in mind, that the word "compel" means to grab hold or to force one's attention. These recommendations are not being made in their order of importance, and could begin anywhere.

Tamas Hacki: *Füttykonzert: Virtuoso Whistling Concert*

In reviewing this recording, the eminent music critic and editor of *Stereo Review* James Goodfriend, describes the effect it had on his little daughter: "After hearing, unannounced, about three measures of this disc, my six-year-old daughter tore out of the room and came back banging a tambourine. She danced through both sides of the record while playing, in succession, every toy instrument she could lay her hands on, and then asked to hear it over again." Now that's what we mean by *compelling!* Interestingly enough, the word "inspiration" comes from the same etymological root as "spirit" which means "breath" or "to breathe." See the brilliant Italian movie

Respiro (2002); even with a hangover, you'll be refreshed. According to the ancients, the muses "breathed" life into the imagination and what could be more apt than whistling? What a marvelous convergence of similarities! This recording is also unprecedented Hungarian weirdness, so bizarre that it will jump-start the most hungover morning. Even Lady Brett Ashley of *The Sun Also Rises* would get moving before her usual 5PM wake-up call. Just to hear the *"Triumphal March"* from Aida and Liszt's *2nd Hungarian Rhapsody* whistled is worth the price of the record.

For something less strange yet compelling for very different reasons, we offer you the warmth and security of long past but not forgotten Sundays in the park with the virtuoso Cornet player and renowned conductor, Gerard Schwarz. The recording is entitled *Cornet Favorites* and features classic show pieces of the late 19th and early 20th centuries. Schwarz, ably accompanied by pianist and composer, William Bolcom, performs with obvious affection such charming tunes as Herbert L. Clarke's "From the Shores of the Mighty Pacific," "Sounds from the Hudson," and the incomparable, "The Carnival of Venice" plus many other favorites. The cornet is considerably more mellow than a trumpet, and its darker tone won't exacerbate a headache. Again, it's the "spirit of the breath" (actually identical) that we recommend for its exorcising powers. For more on "exorcism" see Chapter Six.

The last of our sure-bet musical jump starts is any recording of America's first musical superstar: Louis Moreau Gottschalk. We especially recommend the best recording and renditions that we know of his piano music by the superb American pianist, Ivan Davis; and it's called *Great Galloping Gottschalk*. Although many fine pianists have recorded this consistently joyous composer, Davis's performances are the most musically witty that we know. Gottschalk's delightful music will force you to smile regardless of the hangover severity. Your dry mouth may hurt, but you'll smile in spite of the pain. The sweetly melancholy piece, *"The Dying Poet"* will, if you let yourself go, cause you to roll your head gracefully as though swooning, which is what a number of young ladies did when

Gottschalk performed. Like our other unique designations such as "Coziness Quotient" and "Hangover Factor," we offer the general observation that any music that subconsciously induces you to roll your head in a swooning gesture will probably create a soothing effect on your frazzled nerves. So remember the "Swoon Roll Factor" in tailoring your own hangover musical remedy.

We move, now, from dramatic remedies which will empower you to get your day going to more considered, even pre-planned projects ready to be activated the moment you wake up (or come to). Taking our cue from the pioneering studies of Harvard Psychologist, Dr. Howard Gardner, and his *Theory of Multiple Intelligences*, we propose a new designation called "Hangover Intelligence." Dr. Gardner groups intelligence into many varieties, such as Spatial Intelligence (finding your way back to a point of origin in an unfamiliar city) or Interpersonal Intelligence (understanding the nature of groups and spotting the direction of that group). He claims, though, that real learning and, therefore, an accurate measurement of intelligence, can be observed in Project-Oriented behavior, or your ability to carry out tasks successfully.

In short, we are suggesting that you set up as a project the creation of a tape of at least 60 minutes of music that will help you enter the day after a night's overindulgence *before* it happens. We shall offer you our own 90 minute tape (9 selections of about 10 minutes each) of what we consider the ideal kind of music to listen to the day after with short comments on our choices. In some cases we recommend specific performances because of their uniquely soothing qualities.

1. Bach, *"Komm Süsser Tod."* Now, don't laugh, but this is one of Bach's more serene chorale preludes even though the English translation is *"Come, Sweet Death."* Of course, it could fit if you were especially out of control the night before. Try the spectacular gothic organ arrangement by the late, great organist Virgil Fox. Its profundity will overwhelm you. Or, if you prefer a huge, lush orchestral version, Leopold Stokowski's arrangement will transform a gloomy living room into Cologne Cathedral (8 minutes approximately).

If this mode consoles you and you want to stick with it, try Richard Strauss's twenty-five minute elaboration of the same basic theme called *Death and Transfiguration* with special emphasis on the transfigurative aspects of the piece. Few conductors can compete with either Von Karajan's Berlin Philharmonic or George Szell's Cleveland Orchestra performances.

If, however, you want to stay with 8-to-10 minute pieces and would like to add a bit of humor to your A.M., you could follow *"Come, Sweet Death"* with Bach's equally popular chorale prelude, *"Sleepers, Awake!" (Wachet auf!)* as a kind of alternative path to entering your day.

2. Albinoni's *"Adagio"* is a piece whose muted mass will plumb the depths of your feverish soul. We feel sure that Herbert Von Karajan's version with the huge resources of the Berlin Philharmonic will exorcise the poison from your aching loins. Save the chamber orchestra version for normal waking hours (10 minutes). What you need is an ocean of music engulfing you in its luxurious sounds.

3. Pachelbel's *"Canon,"* the piece they played throughout the movie, *Ordinary People*. Again, Von Karajan's huge orchestral version has a better chance of cauterizing wounded cranial membranes than a smaller chamber orchestra rendition.

We suggest 18th century music to start with (with the exception of Richard Strauss) because it has melodies, clear development, and a comforting sense of order. These pieces constitute our version of a musical Commanding Presence and also serve as examples of "Hangover Intelligence" which we urge you to emulate (6 minutes).

Part of what we have termed "Hangover Intelligence" is your willingness to prepare similar kinds of musical projects before the fact, as it were, to have ready if and when you need them. Of course you can always listen to your pre-planned tape without a hangover so that it is an all-purpose project. According to most educational psychologists, one of the measurable components of intelligent people is their ability to imaginatively project into the future, predict results, and plan accordingly. But even if you didn't plan on overindulging and it comes as a complete surprise (which is actually what happens to most normal drinkers), you'll have it ready.

4. By this time you may be prepared for something a little more sprightly yet still thematically appropriate such as Gluck's *"Dance of the Furies"* from his ballet suite *Orpheus.* A minor but nasty pack of mythological deities, the Furies were the "spirits of punishment" whose major target was the mind. Sound familiar? The mode is still 18th century order, yet its quick tempos and pleasing themes will get you moving into the dance of life. Motivated always, of course, by a healthy bit of remorse. For a change of tempo and mind set, play the next section of the ballet called *"Dance of the Blessed Spirits"* (11 minutes).

5. You're probably ready, now that Gluck has prepared you, for some serious sprightliness in the form of a few Scarlatti piano sonatas. These are deliciously compact masterpieces that will awaken the foggiest brain with their dance-like rhythms and simple themes. Not many pianists can negotiate these challenging pieces easily, but we highly recommend the phenomenal performances of the great Maria Tipo on a recent EMI CD. A ten-minute selection will do, but once you start listening, you may have difficulty stopping (11 minutes).

6. We're now tentatively leaving the safety of the 18th century and moving to some romantic selections, beginning with a lovely but subdued piece. We recommend, after the bracing Scarlatti, a serene piano selection by the French composer, Cesar Franck, called *Prelude, Fugue and Variation* in either an organ or piano arrangement, though we think the piano one more charming. Difficult as it is to describe music and its effects, this immediately engaging piece will pacify you with its sense of healing serenity. Franck was a deeply spiritual composer and much of his music expresses a mystical quietism. As the artist and writer, Jean Cocteau, said about the various effects of great music: "Music is not always a gondola, a race horse or a tightrope. It is also sometimes a chair." And on some "mornings after," a few quiet musical chairs will fit the bill. We recommend an inexpensive Naxos CD of Franck's piano music by a wonderful young English pianist named Ashley Wass.

7. This next choice is our musical equivalent of "silly" music, amusing in a very literal way. Camille Saint-Saëns' outrageous piece called *"Etude in the Form of a Waltz,"* a wildly difficult piano virtuoso knuckle-buster, could easily have been the theme music for *La Cages aux Folles*. Remember that the French practically invented High Silliness and Saint-Saëns was their silliest composer (10 minutes).

8. The Germans, too, had composers who occasionally sounded silly, and few were sillier than Felix Mendelssohn especially when he had to compose an overture to a drama he detested. We suspect that he took his revenge on Victor Hugo's *Ruy Blas* by composing one of the most melodramatic overtures in musical history. But it sure does delight the ear and get the listener going. It's one of those pieces that will make you smile. If there were a German Carmen Miranda, she would have written this vampy overture (8 minutes).

9. Unquestionably, the wittiest composer we know is the effervescent Italian, Gioacchino Rossini, the 19th century composer of many delightful comic operas. However, his overtures will wake the dead especially the famous *William Tell*. We don't recommend that one because it's too frantic à la Dagwood Bumstead running for the bus. Rather, we suggest two in particular: the overture to *The Voyage to Rheims* and the overture to *La Gazza Ladra (The Thieving Magpie)*. Their zippy and irrepressible humor will get you up and at 'em regardless what time you got to bed. Stanley Kubrick used *La Gazza Ladra* throughout that strange movie that should *never* be viewed with a hangover, *A Clockwork Orange*. So if the flashbacks from the film are too persistent, try the equally comic *Voyage to Rheims*. George Szell and the Cleveland Orchestra are hard to beat in this crackling repertoire (about 8 minutes each).

We have finished our classical taping project and the product comes to just about 90 minutes give or take a minute or two. You're welcome to ours or you can compose one of your own using some or all of our general recommendations.

Before moving on to our recommendations of Jazz, Pop and Rock Music, we'd like to offer a few general comments on larger musical selections and a few, we hope, amusing anecdotes. We're also listing the Top Ten complete classical pieces that meet our criteria as ideal listening experiences, which may ameliorate the aftermath of the "metaphysical hangover."

A general guideline that can apply to most classical selections is that the music should, preferably, be in a major rather than a minor key. The major keys are brighter, more positive and uplifting than minor keys, which tend to express darker and more serious emotional states. In keeping with that guideline, we recommend all the even-numbered Beethoven symphonies because they are in major keys and experiment less with newer, more romantic innovations:

Beethoven's Symphony No. 2 in D major—a bright, nimble, straightforward account of youthful vigor.

Beethoven's Symphony No. 4 in B flat major—Berlioz loved this work's heavenly sweetness and buoyancy.

Beethoven's Symphony No. 6 in F major—the famous "Pastoral" symphony in which the woods and rocks speak to our souls.

Beethoven's Symphony No. 8 in F major—sometimes called the "Olympian Symphony" which expressed the composer's "aufgeknopft" or "unbuttoned high spirits."

Beethoven's Third, Fifth, Seventh, and Ninth Symphonies are in minor keys and are all brand new developments. They come at the listener with a brashness that could agitate rather than soothe. The relentless repetition of both the *Fifth* and the *Seventh* Symphonies could turn into a case of aural "dogs' eyes syndrome" which pulls you into the repetition unprotected by recognizable form. After listening to many complete recordings of all Beethoven *Nine Symphonies,* we suggest the lively and *buoyant* recordings by the Dresden Philharmonic conducted by the late Herbert Kegel.

After surveying a huge range of classical selections, we have agreed that the single most helpful piece of classical music to listen to under hangover conditions is Bizet's *Symphony No 1 in C major.* Written by the 17-year-old Bizet in a month, it embodies the freshness, charm, and melancholy that most of us lose when we turn 18. The *Andante* movement is one of the most gorgeous pieces ever written. It was used quite poignant-ly in a lyrical Italian film called *Bread and Chocolate*, a film about poor Italians forced to immigrate to Switzerland and work as waiters and servants to support their families back home. The *Andante* is played as the poor Italians (chocolate) are observ-ing—from their pathetic chicken coop home—the blue-eyed, privileged Aryan youths (bread) enjoying a naked gambol in an Edenic Swiss river.

The remaining nine recommendations are not in order of preference but are sure bets on gloomy mornings.

1. Mozart, *Sinfonia Concertante in E flat major*, K.364 a dia-logue of the soul and the self and a recording that brought Arthur Rubinstein to tears when performed by violinist, Arthur Grumiaux, violist, Arrigo Pelliccia, and conductor, Colin Davis and the London Symphony Orchestra.

The "K" in K.364 stands for a musical scholar named Ludwig Köchel (pronounced "Kershel") who catalogued Mozart's many works chronologically. Scholarly radio announcers will always give the Köchel listing or catalogue number when presenting a Mozart piece and would say some-thing like: "We have just listened to Mozart's Symphony No. 40, Köchel Listing, 550." Well, a regularly hungover friend from Boston who knew neither German nor the works of Mozart was befuddled for years when he listened to a classical music station on hungover mornings and heard the following: "We have just listened to Mozart's Symphony No. 40—*of course you're listening*—550." He also heard: "We're now going to play Mozart's most famous chamber piece *'I'm inclined to knock music'*—*of course you're listening*—525." What he should have heard was, of course: 'We're now going to play Mozart's most famous chamber piece, *'Eine Kleine Nachtmusik,'* Köchel Listing, 525." So much for 18th century German hangover humor! Imagine his chagrin when years later, having learned some German and sobering up, he discovered his mistake.

2. Robert Schumann's *First Symphony in B Flat major* called the *"Spring Symphony."* And it is just that, a springy, invigorating, and ebullient romp through Teutonic forests. German-Romantic-Feel-Good music!

3. Felix Mendelssohn's *Symphony No. 5 in D minor, "The Reformation Symphony"*—A "minor" departure from our usual major keys. Mendelssohn's life was anything but the storm and stress of most malnourished, isolated Romantic artists. He was born rich, had healthy relationships with everybody, and loved life. His 5th symphony called the *"Reformation"* was a tribute to Martin Luther (a serious guy—thus, the minor key), but in your case could apply to your need to reform your behavior of the previous *Walpurgisnacht* (night of the witches' sabbath)!

4. Franz Joseph Haydn's *Symphony No. 96 in D major, "The Miracle."* A Haydn work is a must in the waking hours, and this justly famous late work is no exception. The "miracle" alluded to concerns a potential disaster when a chandelier fell in the hall where it was being premiered. But the audience was so charmed by the work that they had pressed forward to hear better and the chandelier missed them. In your case, though, the piece will remind you to be grateful for the "miracle" of awaking this morning without serious injury. Haydn's works never fail to charm with their wry, energetic humor. A recovering alcoholic friend of mine claimed he never knew what he would do after the first drink. He'd casually tell his wife he was going out to get a six-pack and return three days later followed by a SWAT team. But he's alive to tell the tale and listens to Haydn's 96th symphony a lot.

5. Rachmaninoff *Symphony No. 2 in E minor.* This melancholic Russian composer could write the saddest music, but he could also make it not only bearable but even beautiful. He's the finest "It hurts so good" composer around. This work is long and very emotional, but leaves you hopeful. Just what the doctor ordered. We especially recommend the superlative performance by the great Russian conductor, Yuri Temirkanov and the Royal Philharmonic Orchestra, or Valery Gergiev's intense recording (Philips CD) with his phenomenal Kirov orchestra.

6. Tchaikovsky's *Piano Concerto No. 1 in B flat minor.* The world's most famous piano concerto and with good reason. It has one lush melody after another and climaxes that will lift you out of the depths of Blue Monday. The irresistible

last movement, a Ukrainian folk dance, is genuinely magic music. Try either the classic recording by Van Cliburn or Emil Gilels' recording with the Chicago Symphony Orchestra and Fritz Reiner.

7. Camille Saint-Saëns' *Piano Concerto No. 4 in C minor*. Remember that this composer is a kind of French Carmen Miranda. This delightful work, however, sounds profound, which is a nice way of saying it's shallow. Full of sweet themes and exciting developments in the form of hair-raising pianistic demands, it's fun, fun, fun music that will force you to smile. Try Stephen Hough's recent fabulous recording, the last movement of which will have you marching around the room declaiming victory!

8. Antonin Dvorak's *Symphony No. 8 in G major*. So genial and warm and uplifting and you know that Antonin was such a nice guy. If Monty Woolley or Charles Coburn composed music, it would have sounded like this.

9. For those of you of a more religious bent, there is the incomparable *Mass of St. Cecilia* by Bizet's teacher, Charles Gounod. Somehow Gounod combines a religious feeling with a thoroughly human warmth that cannot fail to pacify a feverish brow. Sublime on all counts. Try reissued EMI recordings conducted by either Georges Prêtre or Jean-Claude Hartemann.

We'll now move, since we have called this a Cookbook, into some serious "cookin'" music, otherwise known as Jazz. The great Clarence Beeks (aka "King Pleasure") defined Jazz and its relationship to language, as "puttin' on the pots." In short, you got "cooked" or "fried" or "sauced" or "stewed" last night, and today you may need something to cool down your baked brains. Nothing could fit the bill as effectively as some "cool Jazz," some serious "cookin'" or "puttin' on the pots." We propose that the expression, "Cool it, Man!" arose out of a situation in which a reasonably sober person is advising an intoxicated or hungover person to calm down because his body is full of alcohol which has created so much heat (cooking the brain) that he's become toxic. Jazz is a healthy, non-toxic (or

"Cool") way of generating heat that needs nothing other than its own excitement.

The range and variety of Jazz artists is immense and depends upon individual tastes, but we are going to offer you a selected list of our own preferences hoping that ours is so subjective that it will somehow turn out to be objective, kind of like the way a democracy works—theoretically, that is.

A word of caution: We generally do not recommend those artists who are highly experimental in the sense of breaking radically new formal ground. Such music is, by its nature and purpose, disorienting and does not reassure or soothe the jangled nerves of most hangover victims. Therefore, serious Jazz aficionados may be perplexed by the absence of such luminaries as John Coltrane, Charlie "The Bird" Parker, Bill Evans, Charlie Mingus, Miles Davis or such deeply disorienting geniuses as Lenny Tristano or Bud Powell. You need all your faculties in good working order to enter their Big Time chaos. We do recommend, however, artists whose major project is non-experimental, though they certainly let their fancy take them on extended flights from time to time.

A PIANISTIC SEXTET

1. For all-round pianistic genius and the technique of a Horowitz, firmly grounded in the Blues, the Bizet Symphony of our Jazz section is Oscar Peterson. Rumor has it that the disintegration of the Soviet empire began at his concert in Tallinn, Estonia, on November 17, 1974. Listen to that extraordinary recording and you may agree. It's called *Oscar Peterson in Russia*.

The following recommendations are not listed in order of importance, but alphabetically so as not to offend devoted coteries:

2. Dave Brubeck—still around and still "cool" as ever. One of the great and permanent Be-Bop artists. His best recordings are from the 50's and can be found on the Greatest Hits albums.

3. Don Shirley—a black, classically trained artist with three earned doctorates. His basic grounding is jazz but he

brings both Western and Eastern culture into his unique arrangements. He mixes Schubert with Cole Porter and the results are as delightful as you may imagine. He had a famous hit in the early 60's called *"Water Boy,"* a piece which goes right through you.

4. George Shearing—According to Jack Kerouac's *On the Road*, this super-cool blind artist helped inspire the beginnings of the Beat movement. That unruly crew came up with the designation "beat" during one of his performances.

5. Teddy Wilson—Benny Goodman's long-time pianist. His fingers could find ways around and through the intricacies of Goodman and produce more than mere background accompaniment.

6. George Winston—a New Age artist who obviously comes from a serious musical background and fuses many kinds of musical genres. Very calming effect.

6a. Special Category—Remember our advice to steer clear of Mexican and Central or South American music? Well, we do have an exception: the Piano Music of the Brazilian composer, Ernesto Nazareth (no connection with the Rock Group alluded to later in the chapter). There are two stunning albums of his Tangos, Waltzes, and Polkas played with controlled verve by one of Brazil's finest pianists, Arthur Moreira Lima. Most of these pieces evoke some serious Swoon Rolls and would rank very high on our "Swoon Roll" index.

SEVEN MAGNAVOCES

1. Ray Charles—This memorable artist combined the jazz idiom and the best of rhythm and blues. A real original, his greatest hits like "Georgia," "I Can't Stop Loving You," and other heart-breakers are perfect for official self-pity sessions. Stick to the mellower items.

2. June Christy—50's ultra-slick in the best sense and very musical. She could do anything with her very flexible voice which could smooth out the roughest edges.

3. Chris Conner—smoky voiced, very sexy sounding lady from the 50's and 60's. Similar to June Christy, but Conner's voice had more heft and subdued sexual danger.

4. Ella Fitzgerald—though gone, she endures as one of the most musically intelligent vocalists. Time seemed to take no toll on her chords. Few could "put on the pots" like Ella.

5. Mel Tormé—the male Jazz vocalist without peer. Smooth, clever, and highly witty singer who could do anything with his richly modulated equipment.

6. Sarah Vaughan—even more of a virtuoso than Fitzgerald when it came to talking back to various instruments in jazz lingo. Few could "sass" as delightfully as this genius.

7. Diana Krall—not only a stirring Jazz singer but a brilliant pianist as well. Sad and *very* cool.

A Musical Miscellany of Instrumentalists: For Specialized Tastes

Sticking to our requirement to be "Cool," such guitarists as Kenny Burrell and Joe Pass are obvious choices. Soothing flutists such as Hubert Laws and veteran Herbie Mann (no relation to Thomas) will pipe you to sweeter pastures. The M&M's Chuck Mangione and Wynton Marsalis provide trumpet playing of consummate skill and a sophisticated mix of classical and popular tunes and techniques. Still soothing after all these years, saxophonist Stan Getz never stopped changing, which makes his fans happy, especially when he performed some Bossa-Nova in one of his later releases. For cool-cool vibes, Red Norvo makes life bearable by mellowizing the most strident hangovers. And if his vibes don't "take," try the ethereal beauty of Andreas Vollenweider's electric harp or the jazz violin of the venerable Stephane Grappelli.

The range of popular and rock music is so vast and multifaceted that we're going to list a few personal favorites and move on to our next chapter which deals with Imaginative Exercises for the Walking Wounded.

Of course, so-called Hard Rock or Acid Rock would be suicidal on mornings after. But if you really want to wallow in guilt, play a few selections from The Cramps' latest album, *Bad Music for Bad People* or for some punk masochism try a group called Ed Gein's Car and their only album (thank heavens!), *You Light Up My Liver.* If you are particularly disoriented today and had a fight with your mate about last night's behavior, sample a few tunes from *Mental As Anything's* first album entitled *If You Leave Me Can I Come Too?* It's up to you and what you think you can tolerate.

We conducted a survey of Pop, Rhythm and Blues, and Country Western single vocalists and several groups and have arrived at some generic but nonetheless excellent combinations of styles that will appeal to virtually all age groups regardless of deep-seated preferences. We don't see how our list could offend anyone. These artists are so well known that very few comments are necessary.

No justification need be made for recommending two outstanding groups who combine mellowness with musicality: Manhattan Transfer and The Eagles. These are very different but equally compelling groups. The same regularly hungover friend of ours who misheard the Mozart Köchel Listings, was equally mystified as to how a group such as The Eagles could have come up with a song entitled "Lion Eyes" (or was it "Lionize?"). Since he obviously never listened to the lyrics, he concocted a number of bizarre mental explanations about the mysterious powers of the eyes of lions and/or the mysterious powers of the verb "lionize." For those of you who are not familiar with this classic Eagles' tune, its actual title is "Lying Eyes" which, along with "Take it to the Limit" and "Hotel California" (which may be about a hangover) are very familiar songs. And with good reason.

For those of you who prefer Country/Western, a genre which includes more than a few songs about getting drunk and feeling remorseful the next day, we highly recommend such multitalented stars as k.d. lang and Randy Travis of the younger set, and veterans Charlie Rich and the legendary Willie Nelson, whose collection of oldies such as *"Georgia,"* *"Stardust,"* and *"Blue Skies"* will transport you into another realm. And, of course, Charlie Rich's famous, *"The Most Beautiful Girl"* seems to be about hangover guilt as are hundreds of other Country/Western songs. Vince Gill's heartbreakers are *very* appropriate for foggy mornings.

Two female singers who have always produced calming

effects are Judy Collins and Joan Baez. Collins' album *Who Knows Where the Time Goes*, particularly her version of *"Like a Bird on a Wire,"* is a heartbreaker of the first order. And, of course, Baez brings with her all the mixture of folk-protest of the Sixties. But for those of you who go back to the WWII years, there is the unforgettable Brit, Vera Lynn, whose rich, clear voice embodied more than any singer of those years, the comfort and hope of a safe homecoming after the war. Her version of *"We'll Meet Again"* could cause a prolonged crying jag for some of you Vets.

For a consummate artist who has universal appeal and whose lyrics are seeringly poignant, nobody is better than Elton John. His *Greatest Hits* albums and especially his suite called *Blue Moves* are required listening on which you will be tested next week.

We would like to conclude this chapter with a straightfor-ward listing of some groups and their albums for four reasons:

1. To make you laugh.

2. To prove our theory that there is such a thing as an inherently "funny list."

3. To amaze you with the incredible range of what's out there to help your condition if used in creative ways.

4. To point out the hidden allusions to the hangover con-dition in one form or another and to support our other theo-ry that in music, as well as literature and media, the "hangover" plays some crucial sub-textual roles heretofore previously overlooked. We would also like to contribute to the proliferat-ing schools of Critical Theory by proposing a kind of semiotic deconstruction of the "hangover condition" as establishing an intertextual reading of most serious creative activities after December 1910 to the present. Say what?

If you recall, there was a actual movie called *The Big Hangover*. Well, we found a musical equivalent. A group called Nazareth actually recorded an album entitled: *Hair of the Dog!*

FIND THE HANGOVER ALLUSION:

Rock Group	Album(s)
Christian Death	*The Decomposition of Violets*
The Cryan Shames	*A Scratch in the Sky*
The Cure	*Happily Ever After; Kiss Me Kiss Me Kiss Me*
The Damned	*Machine Gun Etiquette*
The Dead Milkmen	*Beelzabubba; Bucky Fellini*
Dead or Alive	*Mad, Bad and Dangerous to Know* (a description of the heavy-drinking, famous, and frequently hungover poet, George Gordon, Lord Byron); *Sophisticated Boom Boom*
Defunkt	*Thermonuclear Sweat*
Milky Dread	*Beyond WWIII*
Ethel and the Shameless Hussies	
	Born to Burn
Fiction Factory	*Throw the Warped Wheel Out*
Flipper	*Blow'N Chunks*
The Immaculate Fools	*Tragic Comedy*

For hangover-induced temporary dyslexia, or embarrassing hangover malapropisms:

Incorporated Thang Band	*Lifestyles of the Roach and Famous*
Jane's Addiction	*Nothing's Shocking*
Joy Division	*Love Will Tear Us Apart*
Klaatu	*Klaatu* (watch the movie we recommended called, *The Day The Earth Stood Still* and you'll get it.)
The Leather Nun	*Force of Habit*
Los Microwaves	*Life After Breakfast*
Aida Nova	*Twitch*
Omen	*The Curse*
Nazareth	*Expect No Mercy; 2XS*
Plan 9	*Keep Your Cool and Read the Rules*
The Pogues	*Rum, Sodomy, and the Lash!* (recorded on Stiff Records—no less!)

Poison	*Look What the Cat Dragged In*
Suicidal Tendencies	*How Will I Laugh Tomorrow When I Can't Even Smile Today?*
Tears for Fears	*The Hurting*
Traffic	*John Barleycorn Must Die*
Dweezil Zappa	*Havin' A Bad Day*

Since this chapter is about music cures, we're going to experiment with some international remedies, with special emphasis on Central and Eastern European specialties: Hungarian, Polish, Russian, and Siberian. *Nota Bene!* Anything Gypsy will *always* work.

MENU

"B&S"

1. Have available some simple name-brand vegetable juices; these are often used to palliate the pain of hangover. Clamato juice with a little Worcestershire, pepper, and garlic salt mixed in. It will really perk you up because the taste is a little bizarre and may well produce flashbacks of quaint little neighborhoods in Budapest, even though you've never been there. Since you're in a recognized ASC (altered state of consciousness), enjoy it. An acquaintance who is hungover a lot calls it *Kafkasizing* it, which is a post-modern technique known as defamiliarization; that is, taking the familiar and making it strange, which is *exactly* what a hangover does to most people. Come to think of it, the hangover sensibility may be responsible for postmodernism! Jackson Pollock kept dropping his paint cans! If Clamato juice is too threatening, try V-8 juice or just plain tomato juice with the same added ingredients.

2. But what could be more satisfying or nutritious than cabbage soup! Put on a recording of Emmerich Kalman's *Countess Maritza* (1924) and start puttin' on the pots. First fry the cabbage in bacon grease and then pour it into the broth of boiled corned beef with bits of corned beef floating in it. Add diced onions, potatoes, and celery. Also add small pieces of bacon and celery. Top it all off with a lot of paprika and but-

ter. Get ready for laughing jags especially among a group of equally hungover people who will look at each other and burst into laughter because it is so good even though they were so bad last night. See Chapter Five and the HO laughing scene in Fielding Dawson's novel *It's a Great Day For a Ball Game!* Major survivor guilt! Top each bowl off with some minced parsley and sour cream. If you'd like to add some visuals to the emerging Poe party, watch the move *Frankenstein Meets the Wolfman* (1943) with Lon Chaney, Jr., wreaking havoc in the little Transylvanian village of which police chief, Lionel Atwill, has lost complete control! Where is the Gypsy woman, Maria Ouspenskaya, with the wolfsbane antidote? With those watery eyes and shaking voice she's *got* to be hungover.

"MP&E"

1. My English teacher nephew, Curt Meanor, recommends a southwestern Ohio remedy that came from somewhere near Dayton: sausage sandwiches. Slice up some Jimmy Dean sausage, fry up some patties (in bacon grease) and place between 2 pieces of white toast, add mayo or Miracle Whip. Garnish with potato chips (or French fries) and sweet pickles. If you're feeling particularly bold and puckish, have small olives instead of pickles. What the Hell, go against the grain—like Huysmans and his bejewelled tortoise.

2. Back to our old standby: Bacon. In general, bacon is very popular with the hungover. Fry up a half a pound, cut into small pieces and mix it in with a bowl of Campbell's Navy Bean soup; add the grease. Or fry up enough bacon for a large sandwich. Toast two pieces of white bread, fry an egg over easy, and place the bacon and egg on the toast (one piece). Place the open-faced toast under the broiler after you have added a slice of Swiss cheese (or cheddar) on top, and let it brown or till the cheese has melted. Cover it with mayo or Miracle Whip and get ready to faint from the pleasure. This was my own personal remedy for hangover for the 21 years I endured them. Since I stopped drinking alcohol on July 31, 1977—the feast day of St. Ignatius of Loyola—I still occasionally have this same breakfast for old time's sake. Pepsi or Coke—ice cold—is the perfect accompaniment.

3. For you old classic movie fans, we recommend the "W.C. Fields Sadistic Hangover Cure" from one of his great films, *The Bank Dick* (1940). Fields is suggesting a very specific hangover remedy for a very hungover Franklin Pangborn, a bank examiner. Throughout Fields' cruel recitation of his cure, Pangborn becomes increasingly more nauseous until he is forced to seek refuge in the nearest bathroom. Here is the exact menu Fields is offering to Pangborn: A breaded veal cutlet with tomato sauce; a chocolate éclair for dessert; liver and bacon; or 2 pickled eggs and some castor oil; or Hungarian Goulash and coconut custard pie. Fields is being more than just a bank "Dick" during this very humorous scene!

4. For those of you whose stomachs are very sensitive the next day, we offer the exact opposite menu of Fields' literally sickening remedy. This one is from a highly respectable classic work, *Encyclopedia of French Cooking Today,* under "For a Hangover" (p. 541): "Drink plenty of cold, pure water until your stomach is settled. Then you may take a little clear vegetable broth for lunch. In the evening, more broth, and a dry biscuit. The following day, eat very lightly, choosing broiled foods seasoned with just a bit of unsalted butter. For several days, keep to the simplest diet of grilled meat, boiled fish, and steam vegetables." What fun!

"V&S"
1. Hard-boiled eggs with pickled beets. Use salt and pepper sparingly.

"F"
Cantaloupe sprinkled with salt, preferably cubed.

"D"
Chocolate Brownies with vanilla (or coffee) Häagen Dasz ice cream.

CHAPTER FIVE: THE READING READINESS TEST

If you're not in the mood for watching TV or listening to music, yet you are able to read words unencumbered by blurred vision or a temporary case of peripheral neuritis, we have sketched out for you a multi-phasic approach to reading. The severity of your hangover, then, will determine what kind of readings you may wish to pursue.

We recommend that you begin with large picture books on art, photography, architecture, or some other topic you find consistently compelling. If, for example, you are a Rock fan, you may want to peruse something like the *Rolling Stone Guide to Rock*. Or if you prefer classical music, a lovely picture book such as the *History of Carnegie Hall* will fit the bill. Photography books are especially recommended, but be sure they are high quality reproductions. The Time-Life collections on anything are always soothing, especially their historical works on the Second World War or their excellent books on foreign countries. Books on French and English Gothic Cathedrals have been found to be most comforting for their Gothic reassurance.

We recommend top photographers such as Stieglitz, Moholy-Nagy, Steichen, or Cartier-Bresson for slice-of-life scenes. But for photographs that capture that unique quality of the American Sublime (an ameliorative experience always!), no one can surpass Ansel Adams' pictures of the West and Southwest. You must use selective editing, though, when viewing photographs by the great Richard Avedon, particularly his stark images of hopeless people. Even if you didn't have a hangover, they would be more than a little disturbing. In your delicate condition, however, you'd best avoid them, especially his *The American West*. And definitely stay away from any of Diane Arbus' demented-looking Coney Islanders or Bronx giants. Few artists have dared to go near such subjects, but if you do, be prepared to pay the price. Perhaps the most soothing single volume of photography would be the heart-warming *The Family of Man*, a staple of coffee tables for the last thirty years featuring inoffensive, sometimes humorous collections underscoring the myth of the melting pot and reassuring the reader that "God's in his heaven—all's right with the world." Its classic cover of two little children—a boy and a girl holding hands coming out of the woods—says it all! The Big Bad Wolf did not get them … this time, anyway.

In keeping with our consistent emphasis on the soothing effects of "coziness" in any form, page through issues of *Architectural Digest* and *House and Garden* to see and envy how the privileged live. But the volumes we recommend most highly are back issues of *Life* magazine and *National Geographic*. They combine superb photography with bits of nostalgia. Also recommended are large coffee-table books on Hollywood. Crown Publishers put out five gorgeous four-hundred-page books on the five major movie studios: MGM, Warner Brothers, Universal, RKO, and Columbia—so you can spend the afternoon exploring these endlessly engaging goldmines.

If, however, you'd like to move into a slightly more challenging artistic area, we recommend art books that are slightly off center; that is, they stress the remote, idealistic, or the exotic in some controlled form. The Victorians were particularly apt at producing idealized scenes of ancient cultures. Lawrence Alma-Tadema's paintings of ancient Greek and Roman life graced millions of high school history and literature books and would probably be instantly recognizable. He was able to produce scenes that, though realistically vivid, also combine a dream-like quality with little batsqueaks of sexuality. And nothing is quite so disturbing as a combination of the slightly fantastic with the demurely suggestive. Just a tiny show of thigh here or a mysterious lump there could add a little erotic spice to a gray afternoon.

The other English Victorian, even more recognizable, is the renowned Edward Burne-Jones who became famous for his highly romanticized paintings and stain glass of various characters out of the *Legends of King Arthur* and the *Knights of the Round Table*. Most of his subjects are ethereally handsome and even the bad guys look virtuous and inviting.

However, the most captivating of all of these artists and the one who will undoubtedly sooth you most effectively is the modern American painter, Maxfield Parrish. The child-like wonder his work presents may help pull you out of hangover heaviness. They depict settings that embody childhood innocence and a way of life before the Fall. They are idealized versions of the American Eden. His illustrations for children's books such as *Snow White* and *Winken, Blynken, and Nod* and many other classics will leave you breathless. But his series of paintings from 1954 to 1963 that included *"Little Stone House"* must qualify as the perfect combination of domestic and natural tranquility par excellence. Beside his work, Norman Rockwell's books are brutally realistic. However, we also hope to provide you with various landscapes of serenity from the French Gothic of Chartres and Notre Dame to those domesticated Thanksgiving Dinner scenes of Rockwell. Needless to say, any of the rustic/cozy paintings of safe, Edenic domestic settings by Thomas Kinkade are *ideal* for hangover mornings. Stare at them for as long as you can and take deep breaths.

For those of you who wish to take a few intermediate steps towards actual reading rather than basic, non-linguistic visual perusal, we suggest a great favorite among hangover victims: Map Reading. Maps are absorbing under any condition but can be particularly helpful in focusing one's attention on visualizing where things (including you) actually are. One of the hangover's most disturbing side-effects is a form of dislocating vertigo. Your sense of place may be so fractured that even though you "know" where you are geographically, you feel as if you are either in a slightly threatening foreign land, like Albania, or in a dimension somewhere between place and space. So it's important that you observe on a map a mark that designates where you are with a name attached to it. Oddly enough, it can be a calming experience.

A highly sensitive artist—a friend of ours who frequently suffered panic attacks particularly when hungover—found a foolproof method of controlling them by grabbing the nearest ball-point pen and carving his first name on a large paper plate with great force over and over and over—one version on top of the other: *Peter—Peter—Peter* and so on until the attack ceased. Like a terrified victim in a Poe story who fears he may disappear, Peter established his presence and identity by this decisive existential act. Another form of existential terror is the persistent fear that you may fall out of a window (exacerbated, of course, in tall buildings) and/or actually off the planet. Its opposite condition, which we call the "Chicken Little Syndrome," is the fear that the sky, and everything else, will fall on you. So, on mornings when your fears of falling or being cosmically smothered are vying for your attention, you can study maps and locate yourself in an actual world that is waiting for you to re-emerge when you're feeling better. The more specific the map the more reassurance you will receive. As an added benefit, you are also learning to read words again.

Now that you are able to read without great discomfort, we suggest some simple practice sessions starting off with short, concentrated selections. A favorite of many is the *World Almanac, The Information, Please Almanac* or any number of similar compilations of FACTS. You need FACTS today, evidence that there is a world out there that is measurable geographically, historically, and statistically. To read the history of, say, France, in several paragraphs is a sobering experience, or to study the long list of Papal succession or the genealogies of the royal families of France or England re-instates a sense of order in the world which may seem distinctly chaotic in your present condition. There is a place called "France" and there are 60 million souls there and possibly 10 million of them may also be hungover today too. So you are not alone!

From almanacs you may want to move on to something a bit more comprehensive such as the fascinating *Time Tables of History*. This product of German scholarship with a vengeance, gives you the major significant events that happened by the year since 4241 BC and divides history up into seven areas such as History/Politics, Literature, Religion/Philosophy, Visual Arts, Music, Science/Technology, and Daily Life. You have all the information you need on a map-like page and can examine the facts endlessly. Facts are even more compelling when arranged in such a way that visual comparison is made easy.

Those of you who may want to look at facts in a more specific way can choose something you are more interested in.

If you are a music lover, the *Schwann Catalogue* (now called *Opus*) a listing of all the records and CDs available, could easily take up several hours and distract you from your condition. Sears' or Penney's catalogues will serve the same purpose, and the models are always fun to look at and wonder about what their life could be like. Also buy Halliwell's *Film Goers and Video Viewers Companion,* an indispensable volume which will tell you what films your favorite actors were in and if they're still around. Check out a section entitled "Drunk Scenes," which is a detailed listing of the most famous ones. This book even lists two great scenes of Laurel and Hardy getting drunk: *The Bohemian Girl* (1936) and *Scram* (1932). Also Lucille Ball in *Yours, Mine and Ours* (1968). Her drunken question "Who dat!" will break you up like no other scene we can remember.

Moving from basic books to works specializing in even more specific information, you could spend many hours looking through something like Leonard Maltin's informative *TV Movies and Video Guide*, which devotes a small but comprehensive paragraph on just about every movie ever made, 1222 pages of informed opinion. Even more effective would be a combination of watching the movie and reading about it in a film guide of this sort. Such an activity can double the pleasure of the experience and lessen your discomfort because you're watching, listening, *and* reading. The more senses involved, the fewer the possibilities of losing concentration and re-focusing on your pain rather than your potential. Remember, it's up to you!

Other reference books can also be used for pleasure. Dictionaries, especially those with illustrations such as the *American Heritage Dictionary,* transform what is usually viewed as a boring routine into a genuinely entertaining and educational exercise. Whoever chose the illustrations for this outstanding dictionary had a subtle but keen sense of humor. See, for example, the figure obviously taken from a medieval manuscript of "a Fool." Yes, they actually found an illustration of a genuine fool. This dictionary has also put in pictures of plants or animals whose names you've seen many times but had no idea what they look like. See what an "aspidistra" actually looks like on p. 78. Or look at the two illustrations of both a woman's and a man's "redingote" to show the differences. Look it up and enjoy random roaming in the *American Heritage Dictionary*. Sadly, and probably due to political correctness, there is no longer an illustration of a "Fool" in the Fourth Edition—the initial reason I bought that wonderful dictionary's First Edition. However, the beatifically gorgeous color photographs in the Fourth Edition will distract you for at least an hour or so. Check out the painting of a "phoenix" by Ben Shahn on page 1320.

Specialized dictionaries on the surnames of a particular country are also recommended. A work such as MacLysaght's *The Surnames of Ireland*, where you can look up your family name and its geographical source can occupy you for an hour or so. Since the synapses of your brain are working in unusual ways, let them guide you where they may, keeping in mind that the hangover condition qualifies as a genuine altered state of consciousness (aka ASC) and could unexpectedly chance upon strange associations and surprising connections. Maybe there was something in the water on the family farm in County Mayo that predisposed you to getting these vicious hangovers.

There is no question that much of modern American, Irish, and British literature was probably written with a hangover. Remember that authors such as Ernest Hemingway, Sinclair Lewis, F. Scott Fitzgerald, Sherwood Anderson, John Steinbeck, and many, many others were heavy drinkers. To confirm this theory compare the dark, depressingly bitchy *Diaries* of the distinguished British author, Evelyn Waugh, a man who suffered almost daily hangovers, with his genial and optimistic *Letters* which were often written on the same day. The *Diaries,* it seems, were written in the morning when his hangovers were in full force, while the letters were written later in the day when the hangover had lost its lethal edge. Some literary critics believe that the multiple voices in James Joyce's *Finnegans Wake* were not fabricated; they were "recorded" by the heavy-drinking author as he heard them. Oh, boy! And Stephen Daedalus, one of the major characters in Joyce's

Ulysses, is suffering from a terrible hangover throughout the book.

It's a sobering thought (no pun intended) to realize that these authors wrote wonderful, Nobel-Prize-winning works in spite of their habitual hangovers. One is tempted to ask how much better could they have been without a hangover?

If, however, your languorous searches through such temporarily comforting works such as *The Oxford Dictionary of Quotations*, the *Guinness Book of Records*, or those depressing books called *What Ever Became of…?*, do not adequately displace the condition, then it's probably time to take up major literary works which will, hopefully, provide a fictive covering, a kind of literary prophylactic, that could occupy most of the day. It's vitally important for these books to be readily available so you won't have to go rummaging around for them. We suggest that you reserve a shelf for works specifically designated, just as you have designated drivers, for hangover days. Pre-planning is very important.

Before beginning our recommendations for the most suitable books to read during a hangover, we must call your attention to one of the strangest novels we have ever run across.

In our chapter on *Media*, we alluded to a 1945 movie, *Hangover Square*, starring Laird Cregar. That movie was a loose adaptation of a very fine 1939 novel of the same name. The novel, not the movie, is the single most comprehensive fictional treatment of the pathology of a habitually hungover person that we have encountered. The permanently crapulous protagonist, George Harvey Bone, suffers a 200-page hangover, but the novel's tension evolves from the fact that Bone's hangovers increase in severity from a diminutive "Click!" in chapter one to a resounding "Crack!" towards the end of the book:

> "Crack! ..."
> It had almost knocked him down. It made him reel. It was as though he had been hit by someone. And with the crack, everything came flooding, rushing, roaring back—noise, color, light, the fury of real everyday world... He leaned against a wall, giddy and faint.

That crack! Usually it was a little click, a pop, a snap. But this time his brain had almost burst in two; it had practically knocked him off his feet. These attacks were getting worse. He was an ill man."

Hangover Square or *"The Man with Two Minds"* p.181

Of course, the click moves from snap to crack and finally to Pop! and George Harvey Bone brutally murders his slutty alcoholic mistress and her British Fascist buddy, appropriately named Peter, with a 7-Iron. This is definitely not the book to read with a hangover.

THE TRINITY: OUR THREE BEST HANGOVER READING RECOMMENDATIONS

It is virtually impossible to rank the first three in order of importance; that's up to you. But we are convinced that more than a little relief from your discomfort will result once you enter into the magic world of these unique books.

G.K. Chesterton's *The Man Who Was Thursday* is an unique literary experience. Nothing approaches its combination of domestic coziness, espionage, mystery, and fantasy. The title sounds as though it came right out of a hangover sensibility since the unexpected last word of the title characterizes the fragmented linguistic pattern many hangover victims experience. When you're not saying two or three words at the same time, you may be unconsciously substituting words from the next sentence. However, the odd use of "Thursday" is part of the unraveling of an unbelievably complex plot that eventually becomes very simple.

The settings out-domesticate even Sherlock Holmes' 221-B Baker Street. Chesterton portrays the quintessential Victorian London at its quaintest: Fleet Street, the Strand, Cheyne Walk where the mini-Gothic houses sit in their dark, inviting warmth. Their interiors look as though they were designed by the Scottish architect, Charles Rennie Mackintosh, with windows and furniture by William Morris, and art deco figures by Eric Gill. The character of Sunday is unlike any other in literature; he is a kind of beatific Oliver

Hardy without the slapstick, someone you would pour out your soul to in great choking sobs.

Chesterton's other novels, particularly *The Napoleon of Notting Hill*, are almost as delightful, zany, and reassuring. His endings are visionary experiences. But as you read more and more of his work, you begin to suspect that he was not unfamiliar with the hangover condition; and if you delve into the biographies, you will find your suspicions confirmed. Nonetheless, his exquisitely spacey sensibility will undoubtedly bring comfort and joy to all readers. *The Man Who Was Thursday* is a work that Stephen Spielberg could make into a spectacular movie. Too bad Stanley Kubrick is dead.

The second sure-bet novel that cannot fail to make you laugh out loud and wish were longer, is John Steinbeck's *Tortilla Flat*. Its episodic structure requires little effort to follow. The characters are an irresistible conglomeration of folks just "hanging out." Most of them don't work on a regular basis, and their principal occupation is sitting around drinking wine, telling stories, and enduring hangovers. It's a less than subtle retelling of *King Arthur and the Knights of the Round Table* with some Greek mythology thrown in. And although there is humor on every page, its theme is a profound one for us Westerners. Yuppies, beware of this book. There are some comic hangover scenes especially on the beach and, like Chesterton, knowing Steinbeck's drinking habits, we suspect that it may have been written with a few.

Tom Wolfe's *The Bonfire of the Vanities* is not only one of the finest American novels of recent years, but is also impossible to put down. It will make you guffaw—to heck with giggling—many, many times. Is there an American writer today with a more accurate ear for the way American English is spoken? And the comic payoff of that kind of linguistic precision rarely surfaces in this age of minimalist linguistic banality.

Most importantly, however, is the fact that THE ARCHE-TYPAL HANGOVER HERO plays the crucial role in this spit-fire novel. No one has captured the searing pain of awakening with a hangover as does Wolfe's introduction of his monumentally hungover hero, Peter Fallow:

The telephone blasted Peter Fallow awake inside an egg with the shell peeled away and only the membranous sac holding it intact. Ah! The membranous sac was his head, and the right side of his head was on the pillow, and the yolk was as heavy as mercury, and it rolled like mercury, and it was pressing down on his right temple and his right eye and his right ear. If he tried to get up to answer the telephone, the yolk, the mercury, the poisonous mass, would shift and roll and rupture the sac, and his brains would fall out.

The Bonfire of the Vanities, p. 164.

This, of course, is writing of the highest order describing the greatest hangover fear of all! It's also an objective correlative of the condition. Wolfe traces Fallow's hangover as it staggers its way through the novel's various Dantean levels. He moves from the terror of possible stroke (p. 210) to the "toxic headache" syndrome (p. 303) to hopeful cures (i.e., chamomile tea?) and a veritable taxonomy of hangover remedies (p. 404). Yet Peter Fallow, whose name embodies his paradoxical identity, role, and function, ultimately rises to the top of his profession by his mulish persistence in spite of his wrecked condition throughout the novel. This is also the novel for people who don't read novels with or without a hangover because, as a young friend of ours stated: *"It's just like watching television!"* In fact, it's so vividly rendered, you don't even have to read it; you can just sit back and watch the words perform!

In two of these novels we have the conventional Commanding Presences of Danny in *Tortilla Flat* and Sunday in *The Man Who Was Thursday* but the twist in *The Bonfire of the Vanities* is that the dramatic action of the novel focuses on the very Fall of the Commanding Presence, a self-proclaimed "Master of the Universe," from his seemingly impervious social position. The other hero is also you, the hungover reader, personified as the Hangover Hero, Peter Fallow, as he pursues, like a harpy of ancient Greece, the arrogant Wall Street Bond Salesman, Sherman McCoy, who's "sure" (-man) he's the "real McCoy."

Moving now from our Trinity of the best Hangover Readings, yet sticking with our Biblical nomenclature for purposes of working a little healthy guilt, we're adding four more under the heading The Four Horsemen of the Apocalypse— that is, four novels whose horse-like strength could pull you through your apocalyptic hangover. You may feel as though the end of the world is just around the corner, but our next four recommendations will pit the energies of your imagination against the sometimes daunting energies of the hangover.

THE FOUR HORSEMEN OF THE APOCALYPSE: OR, THE COMMANDING PRESENCE AS DETECTIVE

We've chosen four legendary detectives from England, France, and both the east and west coasts of America, all of them centered within a strong domestic routine. We'll begin with the father of them all: Sherlock Holmes.

1. THE FIRST HORSEMAN: Arthur Conan Doyle's *The Hound of the Baskervilles*.

James Joyce, in the greatest hangover book ever written, *Finnegans Wake*, declaims that: *"There's no police like Holmes."* And what could be a funnier fusion of both the "commanding presence" and "domestic coziness" motifs as found in the great works of Arthur Conan Doyle himself. Holmes' spiritual center is his home at 221-B Baker Street where he can isolate himself and delve into complex cases as deeply as possible. It might be an interesting project to posit a "Coziness Quotient Factor"; that is, to speculate on the relationship between the comfort and security of the domestic surroundings of the commanding presence and his efficiency and success in solving crimes. All of these detectives and police inspectors do their most significant work in the comfort of their domestic tranquility. Our recommendation for our favorite novel of Doyle's would be *The Hound of the Baskervilles*. It's got not only Holmes' Baker Street digs but the added gothicism of the Baskerville estate on the Dorset moors.

We also favor mystery and detective novels not only because they are quick and easy reads, but also because the experience of a hangover often replicates that of both a mystery and a crime. You may feel guilty the next morning whether you did something disgraceful or not. Part of the mystery of the "day after" will be to discover, if you dare, if you were guilty of some inappropriate behavior. In short, having a hangover is like living in a mystery novel, but you have become, simultaneously, victim and violator, pursuer and pursued. Like many a criminal, the hangover victim sometimes becomes his own worst enemy.

We shall now list three other mystery and detective novels out of our Four Horsemen. Like our earlier Trinity they, too, have been chosen because of their literary merit and similar characteristics: clarity, if not simple plots (it's almost a contradiction in terms to find a simple plot in a work whose subject is complexity), then at least plots whose complications are elaborately lucid. The ideal reader, you, must be able to follow a line, as in a Bach fugue, and feel that it's leading somewhere while maintaining the illusion of order amid chaos. Just like life! The characters must be humanly plausible, the style compelling, and the settings as specific as possible. A bit of humor also helps.

2. THE SECOND HORSEMAN: Georges Simenon's *Maigret and the Headless Corpse*.

Our second recommendation is the renowned Chief Inspector Jules Maigret of the Paris Police created by the master French novelist, Georges Simenon. Chief Inspector Maigret is in charge but maintains his authority with a minimum of control and rarely ever has to overtly take charge. He is, in Paris, a local and highly visible celebrity whose innate modesty makes it difficult for him to enjoy the spotlight. Although raised in a small southeastern French town, he knows Paris intimately, having worked as a cop on the beat in a variety of *arrondisments*. He misses the sleazier Parisian slums.

What makes Simenon's detective novels so compelling is the very specific Paris that Maigret moves within. He ambles about the great city in novel after novel (over 40 of them) clarifying confusion, locating the heart of darkness, and restoring order. He is a sensitive enough human being that associating with the dregs of the Parisian underworld sometimes takes its toll on his emotional life. His quiet, intelligent, and caring wife knows exactly when not to question him about the details of a particular crime and their very quaint apartment on Boulevard Richard Lenoir on the right bank becomes his chief haven of emotional restoration.

If you are one of the few who may not have had the pleasure of experiencing Simenon, we urge you to read a classic called *Maigret and the Headless Corpse*. With your hangover, you may feel like a corpse today and, if you misbehaved or "lost your head" the night before, you might empathize with our headless hero. Well, anyway, this reasonably short, concise mystery novel possesses one of the oldest subjects in the world: a dismembered body. Indeed, entire religions have been founded on such attempts to put a body back together again, from Osiris to Humpty Dumpty. But along with the ancient plot, the novel also features a love affair between a teenage boy and an older woman, a quaint cafe where the proprietor lives in the back behind a beaded curtain—just like in the movies—and a mysterious cat. Maigret, who is always fighting a weight problem, loves to eat and enjoys the delicacies of a variety of Parisian cafes though favoring the Brasserie Dauphine, a veritable home away from home on the *Ile de la Cité*. So, even when Maigret is working, you still have homey restaurants featured in practically all of the novels located in Paris. One of our other suggestions for ideal hangover reading is that you know they're good when they make you hungry. And Maigret's constant foraging will do just that. Try to read him with a good Michelin map of Paris at hand.

3. THE THIRD HORSEMAN: Raymond Chandler's *The High Window*.

If, however, you prefer a little humor in your mystery novels since Jules Maigret is not exactly a laugh a minute, we strongly recommend one of American's best mystery novelists, Raymond Chandler. Chandler will make you, in spite of your Peter Fallow headache, at least chortle. Catch this description of a Mrs. Murdock from the opening of *The High Window:*

I could smell the thick scented alcoholic odor of the wine before I could see her properly. Then my eyes got used to the light and I could see her.

She had a lot of chin and face. She had pewter-colored hair set in a ruthless permanent, a hard beak and large moist eyes with the sympathetic expression of wet stones. There was lace at her throat, but it was the kind of throat that would have looked better in a football sweater … She sipped from the glass she was holding and looked at me over it and said nothing.

No wasted words here, and Philip Marlowe, the enigmatic Hard-Boiled Dick, will as often as not be sharing a hangover with you. He always speaks in specifics and loves exaggerated comparisons. His description of a garishly dressed hoodlum as he enters a bar is: "He was about as inconspicuous as a tarantula on angelfood."

Chandler, though, is weak at plot construction but that could appeal to your fractured consciousness in its present state so you won't have to blame yourself for losing track of the sequence of events. In fact, Leonard Maltin in *TV Movies and Video Guide* claims that the plot got so convoluted during the filming of *The Big Sleep* that Chandler himself didn't know who committed one of the murders. We theorize, though, that the real story is that Chandler, hungover again, was trying to explain to the regularly hungover William Faulkner, the screen writer, something so complex that it simply fell apart. At least that's our theory. And it might be that the star, Humphrey Bogart, who was known to enjoy a jar or two, could have been hungover too. Therefore, we have posited what we call "The Hangover Factor" to help decipher unexplainable breakdowns of all sorts particularly when there are no apparent reasons for anything going wrong. Try it out the next time things fall apart at work and ask, if you dare, the forbidden question: "Whose Got the Hangover?"

4. THE FOURTH HORSEMAN OF THE APOCALYPSE: Lawrence Sanders' *The First Deadly Sin*. (Don't miss the Second, Third, and Fourth Deadly Sin novels either.)

We recommend any of Lawrence Sanders' excellent Deadly Sin novels but find his first the most engaging. The Commanding Presence of all of these novels is Inspector Edward X. Delaney, known as "Iron Balls" among his fellow detectives in the New York City Police department. His home is directly adjacent to his precinct on the upper East side of New York which serves as a classic example of Joyce's "There's no police like Holmes." And the town house is as comfortable and inviting as you'll meet in high-class mystery novels.

An added attraction is, as in the case of Maigret, the presence of food. But here it appears in the form of elaborate, indeed, baroque sandwiches that Inspector Delaney constructs when stress-motivated hunger strikes. What he does with cold pork, scallions, an onion roll, and horseradish borders on the pornographic and so effectively ignites the appetite of the reader that we have included it in our recipe section under the title: The Delaney Sandwich Orgy or an "Over-the-Sinker." Inspector Delaney has been unsuccessfully trying to convince his very health-conscious wife, Monica, that the Earl of Sandwich is one of civilization's more important benefactors.

More significantly, however, is the bizarre plot of *The First Deadly Sin* (Pride, by the way) which involves such titillating motifs as brother-sister incest, midwest sexual repression, a strumpet who becomes a millionaire, and an aging couple who revel in sexual activity of all kinds plus much more. The incredibly complex ratiocination that Delaney relentlessly pursues to nail his culprit will dazzle you and keep your attention regardless of the hangover discomfort. One of the best reads ever! Also, don't miss the other Deadly Sins novels: The Second (covetousness), The Third (lust and lots of sexual dismemberment!), and The Fourth (anger). But don't ever go near that genuinely *great* movie *Seven* with a hangover.

(For an extended analysis of Sanders' mystery novels see my article on him in *Critical Survey of Mystery and Detective Fiction,* Salem Press, 1988, pp. 1460-1466.)

FAMOUS HANGOVER SCENES: MIRROR, MIRROR! WHO'S THE MOST HUNGOVER OF THEM ALL?

Since American literature is full of hungover authors, four Nobel Prize winners and any number of Pulitzer winners, there are, of course, some notable hangover scenes worth mentioning. To conclude our chapter on suggested readings we would like to point out some of the more famous hangover scenes from several of our most respected American and British authors so that you may have a basis of comparison of your own.

Perhaps the most amusing hangover scenes come from one of American literature's most accomplished writers, John Cheever. In fact, Cheever probably ranks highest for short stories and novels containing seriously hungover characters. His most famous is from his novel, *Bullet Park,* and concerns the Wickwires, a wealthy, perpetually hungover Westchester couple. They usually appear on a Tuesday afternoon, wearing sunglasses, obviously emerging from a lost weekend. More often than not one of them will have an arm or a leg in some sort of sling. We know of no more accurate description of a man awakening in an unbearable hangover condition as Mr. Wickwire starts his day by trying to get out of bed:

> … he puts his feet onto the floor. He groans. He swears. He stands. He feels himself to be a hollow man but one who has only recently been eviscerated and who can recall what it felt like to have a skinful of lively lights and vitals … Feeling himself to be a painful cavity he goes down the hall to the bathroom. Looking at himself in the mirror he gives a loud cry of terror and revulsion. His eyes are red, his face is scored with lines, his light hair seems clumsily dyed. He possesses for a moment the curious power of being able to frighten himself." (*Bullet Park,* page 7.)

Once the shock effect of seeing himself in the mirror abates, Mr. Wickwire "stumbles into the kitchen. He sees the empties on the shelf by the sink. They are arranged like the gods in some pantheon of remorse … Their immutable emptiness gives them a look that is cruel and censorious. Their labels—scotch, gin and bourbon—have the ferocity of

Chinese demons…" However, the funniest section of this classic hangover scene is their backbreaking but successful sexual union on an awful Monday morning when every other kind of activity fails: stumbling out of bed, searching the fridge for ice water, falling back into bed and trying to come to grips with having to go to work in such dreadful shape and, in desperation, resorting to a quickie: "Wracked by vertigo, nausea, and intermittent erections, Mr. Wickwire finally got the 10:15 train into Grand Central" (pages 8-9).

Here, again, if you look into Cheever's life-long battle with the bottle, these scenes may ring true. Cheever did, however, eventually sober up and wrote some of his most enduring works. He could still write about hangovers, though, with vivid accuracy; he obviously had a keen memory.

Another famous hangover scene comes from the highly regarded American novelist, Larry McMurtry. In the beginning of his novel *All of My Friends Are Going to Be Strangers* there is a quasi-comic confrontation between a balding middle-aged, desperate but manipulative sociology professor and the young hero's girl friend. The professor creates an enormously embarrassing scene the morning after, pulls rank on and verbally abuses several of his students with whom he partied the previous evening. This is hangover chutzpah at its most controlling. Here, the scene could be merely depressing, but McMurtry's deft hand makes it humorous.

But for the most impeccably rendered recovering scenes in modern American literature see some of the stories and novels of one of our finest writers, Fielding Dawson. They're magnificent in their ability to celebrate sensual pleasure as few authors can. In his *It's a Great Day For a Ball Game!* a randy but very hungover couple are preparing a chicken dinner in the early evening the day after a bout of heavy drinking. The food is so tasty and they are enjoying it so much that they can't stop laughing at each other throughout the meal. You get a sense of grateful relief that they made it to this feast in spite of the previous evening's suicidal imbibing. The consciousness of their survival has transfigured them into happy children enjoying their mushroom chicken in a quasi-hysterical mode.

British literature also has contributed its share of famous hangover scenes, but we have found none that portrays them with such witty accuracy as the opening of Chapter Six in Sir Kingsley Amis' hilariously satiric novel on British academic life, *Lucky Jim:*

> Dixon was alive again. Consciousness was upon him before he could get out of the way; not for him the slow, gracious wandering from the halls of sleep, but a summary, forcible ejection. He lay sprawled, too wicked to move, spewed up like a broken spider crab on the tarry shingle of the morning. The light did him harm, but not as much as looking at things; he resolved, having done it once, never to move his eyeballs again …

Who, but our own Tom Wolfe, could approach this kind of flawless description?

Satiric novels do not, as a rule, go over well on hangover mornings, but *Lucky Jim* is so tastefully presented, we think it may be the only exception and, therefore, enthusiastically recommend it.

However, if you're not ready for British satire and would prefer a novel in which the hangover plays an active role in the main character's behavior, see F. Scott Fitzgerald's *Tender is the Night.* As Fitzgerald himself put it: "The hangover became part of the day, as well allowed for as the Spanish siesta." This is certainly one of Fitzgerald's most brilliant novels and traces his personal descent into the maelstrom of his own alcoholic demise. Not a light book by any means, but a grimly perceptive reminder of what habitual overindulgence can do.

We may have mistakenly suggested by our examples that the hangover is a topic that has only recently been recognized in modern or contemporary literature. Not so. Alexis Bespaloff in his charming book, *The Fireside Book of Wines: An Anthology for Drinkers,* quotes copiously from such Ancients as Plutarch, Xenophon, and the Bible to classic 17th., 18th., and 19th. century authors: Robert Burton, Charles Lamb, Samuel Butler, and the principal scribe of neo-classical Hogarthian excesses,

James Boswell. Boswell's major projects were recording in his *Journals* the conversations of Samuel Johnson, enduring the painful effects of VD, and drinking to excess. His ability to document with frightening objectivity his own drunken behavior and hangovers are unique in the annals of literature. His description of the end of a drunken debauch and the disastrous day-after are worth quoting:

> FRIDAY 10 November.
> But when I got into the street I grew very drunk and miserably sick, so that I had to stop in many closes in my way home, and when I got home I was shockingly affected, being so furious that I took up the chairs in the dining-room and threw them about and broke some of them, and beat about my walking-stick till I had it in pieces, and then put it into the fire and burnt it. I have scarcely any recollection of this horrid scene, but my wife informed me of it.
>
> SATURDAY 11 November.
> My intemperance was severely punished, for I suffered violent distress of body and vexation of mind. I lay till near two o'clock, when I grew easier, and comforted myself by resolving vigorously to be attentively sober for the future. There is something agreeably delusive in fresh resolution.
> James Boswell, *Journals*

Plutarch, the first-century Greek biographer and possessor of judgmental attitudes rivaling the sternest New England Calvinists and making even Jonathan Edwards seem morally soft, graphically berates heavy drinkers for their sexual impotence:

> Now the great drinkers are very dull, inactive fellows, no women's men at all; they eject nothing strong, vigorous, and fit for generation, but are weak and unperforming, by reason of the bad digestion and coldness of their seed. And it is farther observable that the effects of cold and drunkenness upon men's bodies are the same,—trembling, heaviness, paleness, shivering, faltering of tongue, numbness, and cramps. In

> many, a debauch ends in a dead palsy, when the wine stupe-
> fies and extinguisheth all the heat.
>
> Plutarch, *Morals*

We searched high and low for poems that we might add to our lists and found two lovely ones by the late American poet, James Wright. And, just as there was a movie called *The Big Hangover* and a rock album entitled *Hair of the Dog,* James Wright wrote two poems called: *"Two Hangovers."* One of these poems describes a major spiritual experience that the victim is having in spite of his hangover condition. Wright is a wonderful poet for any frame of mind.

The unquestioned King of Hangover Sensibility, though, is America's most popular poet, Charles Bukowski. His twenty volumes of poems, 5 novels, and 6 collections of short stories contain some of the most vivid hangover scenes in American literature. His screenplay for the underground classic, *Barfly,* starring Mickey Rourke and Fay Dunaway, also qualifies as one of the few dramas that demonstrates the triumph of creative persistence during a series of devastating hangovers. In spite of the general gloom of his narratives, Bukowski can make you laugh at yourself (even with a hangover) as few writers can because of the utter honesty of his perceptions and total lack of self-pity. We particularly recommend his terrific collection of poems, *Love is A Dog From Hell* (1977) and his thinly veiled autobiography, *Ham On Rye* (1982). See my article on Bukowski's novels in *Magill's Survey of American Literature,* Salem Press, 1992 (pages 290-301).

After a few reading-related recipes, we now move on to our chapter on Imaginative Exercises; that is, our plan for syn-thesizing a number of our suggested remedies into new and creative combinations, an opportunity for you to use your imagination as it may have been sparked by some of our offer-ings. This is the final C of our Four-Point Plan, the Fourth C for Creativity—which is what this book is really about.

MENU

"B&S"

1. Here's a very specific remedy from a famous person. It's called "The Bill W. Hangover Treatment"; I hesitate to use the word "cure" because, as some of you may know, the AA Fellowship doesn't believe in a cure for alcohol-related problems/issues. But this is what Bill W. (who was the co-founder of Alcoholics Anonymous with Dr. Bob in Akron, Ohio, in 1935) suggested: Give your trembling, hungover sufferer tomato juice mixed with sauerkraut juice and a tablespoon of Karo corn syrup. Talk about a sweet/sour bombshell combo!

2. A less radical treatment would be a traditional standby nostrum: Manhattan Clam Chowder. Choose a good canned selection, like Progresso, because it has plenty of actual clams. But if you want more − and excessiveness is the key in HO remedies—fry up (or broil) some canned clams in butter and dump in the soup. Pour in plenty of soy sauce and that old standby, garlic salt or powder.

"MP&E"

1. One of the most popular (and healthy) remedies for hangover is the King of Hangover Cures: Omelettes! For one thing, they are easy to prepare. We suggest the standard garden-variety ones: cheese, mushrooms, tomatoes, and onions. If you're going to a diner, ask for their Feta Cheese Omelette or, better yet, their Mediterranean Omelette, which is made with Feta cheese, tomatoes, and onions. Add a side order of bacon and enjoy!

2. In our research for this book, we ran across an informative article from *Prevention Magazine* entitled "Vitamins for Sinners." (Nothing like a non-judgmental approach to the problem!) But it does specify the nutritional needs of hangover victims in a quasi-imaginative way. The author of the article suggests taking some extra vitamin C on the morning after, along with foods rich in methionine and cystine, such as cashews, sesame and sunflower seeds, and eggs. We suggest frying up these ingredients and creating a wonderfully healthy and tasty omelette. Call it the "Sinner's Omelette." I'll bet

adding a few mushrooms would add some flavor to it, but you must not enjoy it too much, you Sinners!

3. Here's the novelist Jimmy Breslin's nostrum: cold pizza from the night before.

"F&S"

1. There is a wonderful Irish novelist named Jennifer Johnston who wrote a heartbreakingly poignant novel called *The Captain and the Kings,* about the relationship between a young boy and a lonely old man. As a remedy for a hangover— I forget whose—someone suggests the following: prawns (large shrimp) mixed with mustard, pepper, and garlic salt. Either fry it up in butter or eat it cold in a salad.

"V&S"

1. Fry up some cabbage in bacon grease or butter with pieces of bacon or ham in it. Make a lot of it so you can reheat it that night after the major trauma of the hangover has passed.

2. Egg salad sandwich on whole wheat. Sweet pickles and potato chips. Pepsi or Coke ice cold. Also Dr. Pepper.

"F"

1. Fresh pineapple. Plain or cold.

"D"

1. Hot fudge sundae with walnuts (vanilla ice cream: Häagen Dazs or Ben & Jerry's).

CHAPTER SIX: EXORCISE WITH EXERCISE—
IMAGINATIVE CALISTHENICS

David Outerbridge, in one of the few witty treatments of this condition called *The Hangover Handbook,* proposed three ways of overcoming a hangover:

1. Endure it.
2. Numb it.
3. Eliminate it.

We certainly can't quarrel with his three-fold treatment of the condition. What we would like to add, however, are two additional alternatives that are interconnected:

4. Treat it.
5. Use it.

On hangover mornings you will probably experience some pain and possibly some guilt. If it's bad enough, you may even beg to be shot by your mate, who may be more than willing. Let's assume it's a fairly normal occasion where you find yourself wallowing in guilt, bemoaning your condition, and feeling sorry for yourself. There is, however, an alternative response, one in which you can choose to use the considerable energy that pain and guilt generate to treat your condition. In short: "Physician, Heal Thyself!"

Our approach is based upon the premise that a greater energy source than that produced by pain and guilt is the creative force of the imagination, without which nothing is either planned nor accomplished. Remember Luke Skywalker! *All* human action in some form or another derives from the imagination.

Instances abound, but we call your attention to the legendary example of the Irish writer, Christy Brown, and the triumph of his imagination. His physical condition permitted him to use one, small part of his body, his left foot. But with it he painted hundreds of pictures and wrote five books, one of which was his autobiography, *My Left Foot,* which was made into an Academy Award winner. In short, you use what you have, and what you have today is, as the dentist puts it, "some discomfort."

METHOD: TO EXORCISE WITH EXERCISE

Following our habit of tracking the origins of words back to their source, we made a dramatic discovery: The word "exorcise" and the word "exercise" come from the same basic root. They are practically the same word but for the "e" and the "o." Exorcise means "to expel evil spirits by incantation or oath" from a demonically possessed person, a ritual only an Exorcist, usually a priest, can perform. (There are those battling "spirits" again!) And who would argue that the "distilled spirits" that invaded your helpless soul last night can be the vilest spirits around? The power of exorcism must always, then, come from outside the possessed victim.

On the other hand, "exercise" is "the act of employing, putting into play, or using"; that is, generating physical or spiritual energy from within the self. In short, the power resides "within"; the "exerciser" releases it while concurrently generating more power. There is a physical explanation of: "Physician, Heal Thyself!" That Biblical quotation, by the way, is taken from the Gospel of Luke who was a doctor, so he knew what he was talking about. We simply can't escape that inevitable "spiritual battle" between the invading distilled spirits and your own spiritual or inner imaginative forces. You have but to use your own inner resources to treat the condition, thus creating your own Fifth C: the Cure. It's so Emersonian!

We hope that our little book has helped you find various forms of healing, but we now wish to involve your imagination in a number of exercises in which you actively enlist in your own self-treatment by learning how to tap the inner resources of your imagination.

We had initially labeled this chapter, "Spiritual Exercises," but decided that it sounded much too close to that great document written by the founder of the Jesuits, St. Ignatius of Loyola, an ex-roustabout Spanish soldier from the 16th century. Some of the dynamics of his exercises could apply, however, to our vastly simplified suggestions.

EXERCISE 1: MIXING MEDIA—ART AND MUSIC

Here is an exercise which you could use as a model for tailoring your own.

One of the effects of a hangover is a penchant for aimlessly wandering about the house looking for something, but unable to articulate exactly what it is, or obsessively looking in the refrigerator to somehow verify its emptiness, or flipping through the Yellow Pages. Without a focus, the entire day can be wasted in such vapid behavior.

Try this: Situate yourself in a comfortable chair or the sofa and leisurely page through a collection of Maxfield Parrish paintings while listening to music that would seem to express the same feelings. One possibility would be our good-natured friend, Gioacchino Rossini's music for a ballet called *La Boutique Fantasque (The Fantastic Toy Store)* in which many wonderful toys come to life after the shop closes for the night and dance till dawn. The characters in the ballet are close to some of the fantastic characters from Parrish's paintings. Now, make up your own narratives which connect them while you sip lemon soda water. If you're in an American mood, page through a collection of Norman Rockwell's paintings while listening to any of Aaron Copland's ballets on American themes: *Rodeo; Billy the Kid; Appalachian Spring;* and the *Lincoln Portrait.* But avoid Copland's more modernist compositions such as his piano music, chamber music, or symphonies. Their discord may create just that. Try some Arizona Iced Tea while listening, and don't fight the urge to tap your foot, gently. If, however, your hangover is a relatively mild one, try listening to and following the libretto to one of the world's most charming short operas: Ravel's *L'Enfant et les Sortilèges* (The Child and the Magic Spells). It's a lyric fantasy on what happens in a toy shop after the owner goes home, with a libretto by the great Colette. Now you're listening and actually reading a text. Things are progressing! The perfect drink for this perfect work is Blenheim Ginger Ale.

You are engaging your eyes and your ears, while your imagination is establishing audio/visual connections thus diverting your attention from your discomfort. You've also stopped wandering throughout the house in a slack-jawed stupor. *Voila!*

We respond to any and all stimuli automatically. We exhort, though, creative responses to even the pain of a hangover.

EXERCISE NO. 2: MORE MIXING

Let's try another exercise involving art and music.

As we suggested in our chapter on Reading, sometimes your hangover won't allow actual reading, but is amenable to large books of photography. Try one or several of those huge, heavy photograph books of Gothic Cathedrals from the Middle Ages with spectacular views of Notre Dame de Paris, Amiens, Chartres and other cathedrals while you listen to, say, Cesar Franck's *Symphony in D minor,* the closest musical equivalent to a gothic cathedral we know of. Franck spent thirty-two years of his life as organist of the magnificent French Gothic church of Saint Clotilde in Paris. Try Franck's organ music, especially his *Three Chorales* as recorded by the great French organ virtuoso, Jean Guillou, recorded on the organ of the Basilica of St. Eustache, Paris, where Guillou is organist. However, if you insist on authenticity, look for a recording of all the organ music of Franck performed by Jean Langlais on Franck's own organ at St. Clotilde, where Langlais was titular organist for many years. Let your imagination float freely to fabricate your own narrative with the church as setting and the music providing theme and tone. *Voila again!* A suitable beverage might be blackberry soda water.

Those of you who prefer 18th century music might want to play Vivaldi's *Four Seasons* as you peruse photo books on baroque or rococo architecture and paintings from such churches as the Gesú in Rome, or those marvelous Austrian or Swiss Abbeys at Melk or Einsiedeln. You may respond better to the continuous movement of baroque art and music. After all, motion does purify. Sipping Perrier, the obvious choice, will make the adventure even more sparkling.

EXERCISE NO. 3: MAP READING—MUSIC AND HISTORY

If you're not in the mood for gothic or baroque voyages (your hangover may be gothically baroque enough!), we suggest some serious map viewing, but with a focus. Get out some fine, clear, large Rand McNally maps, or those even more detailed U.S. Geological Survey Maps and put on some traveling music such as Smetana's *The Moldau*. Taking your cue from the music, find the Moldau river on the map and track it from its source to where it empties. Go to your encyclopedia and read up on the FACTS about that river, the other rivers that flow into it, and their sources. Keep Smetana's rich music going and delve into the larger work of which *The Moldau* is but a part, a work called *My Fatherland*. As the next section comes up such as "Sarka," who was a Slavonic Amazon, look up her historical and mythological background. That exercise could easily keep you occupied for several hours during which you may learn something while you have distracted yourself from your distraction. Since the maps and the music started with a river, it would be appropriate to drink sparkling water. Try conductor Paavo Berglund's marvelous recording of the complete *My Country* with the Dresden State Orchestra on a mid-price EMI 2-disk set.

EXERCISE NO. 4: BODY MOVEMENT—ACTING AS IF

Let's say that your attention span begins to falter and you need something a bit more physically involving. Well, you've got the music going and you've learned lots of information about Smetana's music, so why not become America's most renowned conductor of Czech music. This is called "Acting As If." And it's a game most of us play frequently but we play it in a semi-conscious state. "Act as if you are this great conductor and get out your "baton" and conduct the Dresden State Orchestra as it has never been conducted before, right there in your living room.

Young people quite unselfconsciously "act as if" they are wowing 15,000 rock fans with their gyrating guitar riffs (sans guitar, that is!). Indeed, Joe Cocker has made a career out of "faking" a phantom guitar. And "Bill and Ted" of the "excellent adventure" films employ phantom guitar riffs when they wish to metamorphose a hell into heaven. An added advantage to this exercise is that it actually gets your body moving in quasi-orderly movements. The rhythmic motions of your body, "as you lead the Philadelphia Orchestra through a Mozart symphony," creates order where there was but spastic chaos before.

EXERCISE NO. 5: MYTHOPOESIS—INVENTING YOUR OWN WORLD

Of course, your imagination can now take off and begin creating a narrative in which you are one of the world's major conductors, and there is a married woman (or man) in the third row whom you have casually flirted with before, after other concerts, and who is obviously being swept away by the passion of your interpretation. She (he) is without her husband (his wife) tonight and will undoubtedly be coming back stage (in tears, of course) and you just may make the move and so on and so forth. You have used the music and a variety of imaginative elements to create a potentially fascinating story because you're acting "as if."

If you don't feel like conducting today, then perform a piano concerto on the coffee table, keeping the same passional object from being swept away, but now by the intense but casual limpidity of your style and impeccable technique. Who can toss off the monumental complexities of the Rachmaninoff *Third Piano Concerto,* making it look like child's play, yet expressing its heart-breaking melancholia blah blah blah!

We hope that our examples will serve to spark your imagination into creating its own fictions to deliver you from your "inertia." Remember our definition of "INERTIA" from Chapter Two as: "in-art" or "non-art"; that is, lacking the ability to create. This is where the Art of Creative Suffering comes to fruition. Hangover suffering remains just that without the transforming powers of the creative imagination. As the great poet, John Milton, put it: "The mind is its own place, and in itself/Can make a Heaven of Hell, a Hell of Heaven." We feel confident that if you use your imaginative exercises as we have shown you, you will enable yourself to exorcise the demons of Hangover or, as Milton put it: Make a Heaven of Hell."

THE AGONY AND ECSTASY OF HANGOVER RANDINESS— DOMESTICATING HELL

The issue of sexuality is a highly ambiguous proposal on mornings after. For many the idea of any sex in such a condition is clearly preposterous; the headache and shakiness would make performance awkward if not impossible. However, there are those who, possessing a Jim-Morrison-Break-on-Through-to-the-Other-Side mind-set, might welcome an orgiastic dip into some hot sexual activity. Don't forget the persistent Wickwires from Cheever's *Bullet Park*. The hangover condition is an authentic altered state of consciousness and, as such, can incite randy behavior. The nervous system is, after all, in a highly sensitized state and may find sex soothing rather than painful. It surely is a healthier alternative than lying around writhing in pain and moaning in self pity not knowing whether you're coming or going. At least with sex, you'll know you certainly aren't going!

Sir Kingsley Amis suggests that vigorous sexual activity with your partner will tone both of you up physically and metaphysically. However, if you awaken with a stranger, you should probably abstain. We suggest that you find out who the stranger is, propose some harmless tickling games, and proceed from there. If you awaken alone, you may or may not want to, as it were, take things into your own hands. Amis advises abstinence because onanism will increase the metaphysical guilt and shame that hangover can produce. We suggest that solitary sex in such a condition might spark a degree of wantonness that could, if performed quickly and with gusto, liquidate large portions of hangover agony.

Hangover Support Groups—Suffering Together Can be Fun and Productive

Many of our projects and suggestions have been aimed at the solitary or isolated hangover victim, but there are a number of activities that can be done as a group. So one of our suggestions for a project is a Hangover Brunch. Of course, it is to be absolutely alcohol free. The focus should be on nutrition and good, healthy food; many of the recipes could come from our menus at the conclusion of each chapter.

The one rule we insist on in this support group is that any and all blame for your condition must be placed squarely on yourself. It is expressly forbidden to blame mom, dad, siblings, or your mate for anything. You put it in your mouth, slopped it up all night and acted accordingly. There is no such condition as co-dependency in the hangover trauma. Leave it at the door!

The thrust should be task orientated but the Art of Creative Suffering should be central. For instance, the host of the Hangover Brunch should have found out in the course of several earlier parties what each of his/her fellow sufferers prefers the morning after and prepared the menu accordingly. Some common nostrums such as milk shakes (either vanilla or chocolate) should be ever present. What you specifically prepare will depend upon the information you have collected. But the real fun of the brunch is the surprise and gratitude that each participant experiences when he or she is presented with a favorite morning-after food and beverage. Now there's a thoughtful and imaginative host!

One of the games you might want to play at the brunch is ranking or grading the intensity of the hangover by number. You need to openly express your pain and compare it to others. Specific articulations as to exactly how you feel are important in sweeping away any form of denial and will enable everyone to share their feelings. A moderately hungover person might rank himself as a 6 on a scale of 10, but his wife ranks herself as an 8 or 9 because she is having trouble finishing sentences. In Ireland, which is a land where everything is a form of competition, hangover mornings can be spent articulating as precisely as possible just how awful one feels to such a degree that it becomes humorous and people begin laughing. It's a form of relating war casualties and gaining a healthy perspective.

Another task-oriented activity would be that each participant would be responsible for bringing some literary hangover recipe from one of his favorite authors. A fan of Larry McMurtry's works could bring lots of bread and butter and "as much grape jelly as possible," a recipe from his novel *All of My Friends Are Going to Be Strangers.* Or a Lawrence Sanders' fan could provide the fixings for an Inspector Edward X. Delaney sandwich orgy (see the menu at the end of chapter 5) or a veal specialty from Simenon's Inspector Maigret's favorite Parisian restaurant, Brasserie Dauphine.

Any number of variations among these imaginative exercises can be attempted. You could experiment with different kinds of music that might be played during the Hangover Brunch. If you're serving, say, a Polish Salad (see recipe below), probably some Chopin Mazurkas or Polonaises would create an appropriate atmosphere. The important point is to keep your imagination engaged and your body moving.

MENU

"B&S"

1. Apple juice. This is a universal remedy. It is especially recommended by college students for late mornings.

2. Dr. Edward Kelly, who helped organize this book, suggested a Yonkers, New York, remedy: Drink the juice from a can of peas with the peas still in it. And drink it out of the can; don't pour it into a glass, for heaven's sake. Drinking it from the can saves the act from being borderline barbaric, somehow. I guess you have to have a hangover to understand that subtle distinction.

3. In a similar though distant vein, my Siberian friends Yevgeny and Sasha claim that their fellow Siberians' favorite HO cure is drinking dill pickle juice, preferably from the jar with the pickles still in it.

4. Polish Potato Soup: I once worked in a lively Polish

neighborhood in Cleveland, Ohio, at Smerda's Music Store. At Christmas time we went to Linkas' Bar and restaurant for their incredible Potato Soup. I had to bribe the cook for his recipe and here it is: canned potatoes, onions, celery ribs, lots of chicken stock and butter, salt and paprika, a dash of Worcestershire sauce. And then dump in sliced hot dogs, or shrimp, or bits of ham and faint with pleasure.

"MP&E"

1. The Larry McMurtry Texas Hangover Cure: Ham and eggs (fried, over easy) and "all the grape jelly in the place!" This is from a riveting scene in McMurtry's novel *All of My Friends Are Going to Be Strangers*. See our chapter on Reading Readiness for one of the most embarrassing hangover scenes in modern American literature.

2. However, one of the most elegant and easy to fix hangover remedies comes from my dear colleague, Dr. Julia Boken. It's from her Upper West Side of Manhattan, Columbia University environs: baked or broiled salmon and buttered potatoes sprinkled with minced parsley. Have you ever heard of a simpler dish! Schweppes Bitter Lemon might be an appropriate drink.

"S"

1. Waldorf salad: lettuce, bananas, walnuts, and apples.

"D"

1. Manhattan Cheese Cake with vanilla ice cream and strawberry sauce.

CHAPTER SEVEN: THE ST. LAWRENCE MEMORIAL RECIPE— THE STATIONS OF THE COURSE

Those of you familiar with traditional cookbooks will notice that ours includes a limited number of offerings and few specific directions or measurements. We truly believe that the simpler the directions the better, because most victims are in no shape to choose from among many offerings or engage in complex measuring activities. We hope that our lack of detailed explanatory apparatus will simplify food preparation on the morning after and not appear as simple-minded. Our highly selective recipes require a minimum of action, thought, analysis, or measurement. Just do it!

We had originally planned to make the last chapter in the book a listing of over 70 recipes, food and drink that might counter the hungover condition. Instead, we scattered the recipes throughout the book, as chapter endings, the better to serve you early relief. Our approach is, in short, an existential one in which action creates meaning since, in situations of great stress, we often do what we know before we know what we do. So just relax and let us take you on a simple journey through our culinary stations of the course. If you agree with our general philosophical approach, you'll enjoy our next minimalist vegetarian cookbook called: *The Existential Cookbook: Bean and Nothingness,* which will be half the size and even less complex than this one. *Bon appetite!*

Believe it or not, there is a highly venerated saint from the Christian community who is the patron saint of hangover victims. Well, almost. St. Lawrence was a 3rd century Roman martyr who has become famous for the way he was murdered: he was literally roasted on a gridiron over hot coals! He also is reported to have requested after hours over the fire: "Let my body be turned; one side is broiled enough." Now that's, at least, grace under pressure and also demonstrates a stunningly sardonic sense of humor. A genuine Hemingway hero. He has been venerated for 1600 years as the patron saint of burn victims, cooks, bakers, the Poor Souls burning in Purgatory and, oddly enough, librarians!

The connection with the hangover is clear in a number of ways. First off, modern scholars regularly reinterpret ancient stories to update them and make them psychologically applicable to modern times. And it is quite obvious that hangover victims certainly qualify as "poor souls" who are roasting in the cleansing Purgatorial fires of the morning after. Indeed, guilt is traditionally described in fiery terms. And St. Lawrence's timid request, under the most trying circumstances—that he be turned over since he was done on one side—demonstrates a clear case of masochistic behavior; so much so, that he should also be designated patron saint of masochists. And there is little question that hangover victims are seriously engaged in major masochistic behavior(s). His feast day is celebrated on August 10, the day he was roasted and, coincidentally, one of the hottest days in the year.

The Catholic Cookbook describes a tradition on the feast of St. Lawrence of eating cold meats and avoiding baked, roasted, fried, or broiled meat. Indeed, we suspect that broiled meat would be particularly repugnant on August 10 since that was the very word that Lawrence himself used to describe his own fiery demise. We advise our readers, however, that if you must have your broiled filet mignon on this day, at least make sure that it's cooked rare out of respect for the memory of this obliging gentleman.

We would like to showcase the classic hangover recipe from *The Catholic Cookbook,* which prescribes for the feast of St. Lawrence: Gazpacho—what else? (Thank heavens, they didn't suggest turnovers or fritters!)

We also recommend Gazpacho as the most appropriate elixir for hangover mornings since it contains all the ingredients necessary for a healthy and cool start for the day, especially for someone who got fried, stewed, or broiled the previous night.

THE ST. LAWRENCE MEMORIAL GAZPACHO HANGOVER CURE

4 tomatoes
1 sweet red pepper
1 small cucumber
3 tablespoons vegetable oil
3 garlic cloves
1 onion
1/4 cup bread crumbs
1 cup parsley
1 lb. ice
Blend to purée

And now you're ready to offer toasts to the memory of this wonderful saint. Ooops, toast is not the word to use today. Just raise your bowls high!

The *Catholic Cookbook* also offers other recipes we think appropriate for hangover victims broiling in the inner fires of guilt, shame, and compunction and commemorated on October 31, "The Feast of the Poor Souls in Purgatory." They call it "Bread of the Dead" or "Soul Bread." A musical accompaniment might be listening to a recording of Ray Charles singing some suitable "soul music" classic like "Crying Time." They also suggest as an alternative to "Bread of the Dead," a curious dish called "Almond Gruel" which sounds vaguely like something out of *Oliver Twist*.

Most of the recipes in this fascinating book fit the religious feast day quite well, but some have left us puzzled. We wondered why they suggest "Apple Fritters" for the feast of the Ascension or "Nut Sponge Cake" on the feast of Pentecost. The Ascension is the day that Christ bodily ascended into heaven, and Pentecost commemorates the visitation of the Holy Spirit to the apostles who were hiding out from the same kind of soldiers who stewed St. Lawrence. The Holy Spirit descended on them in the form of tongues of fire penetrating their heads and causing them to speak in many different tongues. We'll just let that one alone for now.

Another illustrious saint is St. Anthony of Padua whose

feast is celebrated on June 13th. We propose. him as a minor hangover patron since he is, among many things, the patron saint of "Lost Objects" (like your mind from last night!). There is a recipe for "St. Anthony's Bread," which has become another name for money taken up and distributed to the poor on his feast day. Maybe that's where the Mafia borrowed the term. In any event, *The Catholic Cookbook* offers a recipe for this venerated saint called "Skewered Beef Roman Style," a tasty preparation that we suggest would be more appropriate for the feast of St. Sebastian, a fellow Roman of St. Lawrence who, 28 years after Lawrence's fiery demise, was unceremoniously skewered by the arrows of the Mauritanian archers of that sweetheart Emperor Diocletian. Or perhaps: "Shish Kebab à la Sebastian"?

Just as there are movies and novels called *The Big Hangover* and *Hangover Square,* and three authentic literary hangover heroes, Peter Fallow from *The Bonfire of the Vanities*, history instructor James Dixon from *Lucky Jim,* and George Harvey Bone from *Hangover Square,* there is also a specific dish that was created solely to treat the hangover. Mr. Lemuel Benedict, who was a guest at the old Waldorf Hotel in New York City in 1894, arose one morning with a dreadful hangover. Using his imagination, under the considerable pressure of a hangover, he invented a breakfast that he felt would best treat the condition: Poached eggs on ham or Canadian bacon covered with hollandaise sauce on toast. The chef at the Waldorf was so impressed with its effects that he named the concoction after Mr. Benedict and we have a favorite dish for hangover victims: Eggs Benedict.

BIBLIOGRAPHY

Amis, Sir Kingsley. LUCKY JIM. New York: Viking, Compass Books, 1958. *For one of the great hangover scenes, see the opening of Chapter Six.*

ON DRINK. New York: Harcourt Brace, 1970. *This very witty and sophisticated book contains, perhaps, the classic essay called "The Hangover" (pp. 88-99). Besides providing us with the concepts of the "Physical" and "Metaphysical" hangover, he also prescribes unique selections on both hangover reading and hangover listening. His reading suggestions tend more towards British mystery and adventure writers such as Dick Francis, Eric Ambler and Ian Fleming. He also prefers music a bit more Romantic than what we offered: Tchaikovsky's Sixth Symphony (The "Pathetique"), some lovely Sibelius, and Brahms' Alto Rhapsody, sung by the exquisite Kathleen Ferrier. He does suggest Miles Davis as a reaction formation to the hangover condition, i.e., "if you feel that life is gloomy now, just listen to Miles Davis show you gloominess you never dreamed of!" Be(double)ware, though, of John Coltrane: You're asking for it now!*

Bespaloff, Alexis, ed. THE FIRESIDE BOOK OF WINE: "AN ANTHOLOGY FOR DRINKERS." New York: Simon and Schuster, 1977.

Cheever, John. THE JOURNALS OF JOHN CHEEVER. New York: Knopf, 1991. *For a comprehensive survey of hangover agony at its most vivid, this is the bible of them all.*

Gilmore, Thomas B. EQUIVOCAL SPIRITS: ALCOHOLISM AND DRINKING IN TWENTIETH CENTURY LITERATURE. Chapel Hill: University of North Carolina Press, 1987. *A comprehensive analysis of alcoholics writing about alcoholism: Fitzgerald, Cheever, Waugh, Berryman et al. A definitive bibliography on the illness.*

Hamilton, Patrick. HANGOVER SQUARE: "OR THE MAN WITH TWO MINDS." New York: Random House, 1941.

Karpman, M.D., Benjamin. THE HANGOVER. Springfield, Illinois: Charles C. Thomas Publisher, 1957.

Kaufman, William. THE CATHOLIC COOKBOOK. New York: The Citadel Press, 1965.

Meanor, Patrick. JOHN CHEEVER REVISITED. New York: Twayne-Macmillan, 1994. *The only critical study using information from the letters, the journals, and the biography by Scott Donaldson. See especially chapter eight: "One Day at a Time: the Letters and Journals."*

Outerbridge, David E. THE HANGOVER HANDBOOK. New York: Harmony Books, 1981. *Intelligent, funny, and informative.*

Wolfe, Tom. THE BONFIRE OF THE VANITIES. New York: Bantam Books, 1987. *One of the most entertaining and well-written novels that we have come across. The anti-hero, Peter Fallow, a perpetually hungover, empty British Yuppie becomes the first official Hangover Hero in American literature.*

An Afterword to the Wise

In this age of both alcohol and drug awareness, we wish to point out that this small book is for the normal drinker who occasionally experiences a hangover. The vast majority of drinkers don't intend getting drunk; it usually happens when they're involved with family, friends or fellow workers and not paying attention to how much they're drinking. This book is for them. It is decidedly not for alcoholics or problem drinkers, nor does it in any way promote irresponsible drinking. It is neither for nor against drinking; it deals, we hope, in imaginative and humorous ways of treating the results of overindulgence which a normal, responsible drinker might occasionally experience. We certainly do not want to appear, for some bizarre reason, to promote hangovers. Think of our book in the same way that you think of aspirin or sunburn lotion, which do not promote headaches or sunburn but, rather, treat the effects of these maladies.

If, however, you or a spouse, or child, or a friend is experiencing hangovers on a regular basis which are interfering with any important part of your life/their lives, we suggest contacting any number of organizations or fellowships that address these compulsions in organized, intelligent, and compassionate ways. For those who have a desire to stop drinking but cannot, go to a local meeting of Alcoholics Anonymous. You will be treated with kindness and consideration. For those of you whose spouse, child, or mate is in trouble with alcohol, go to Alanon, a group of sympathetic fellow victims who will tell you exactly what you can and cannot do for your situation.

P.M.
Oneonta, NY
31 July 2004

Patrick Meanor, Ph.D., has not had an alcoholic beverage of any kind for 27 years, but has a very keen memory for pain. He is Distinguished Teaching Professor of English at the State University of New York, College at Oneonta, where he has taught for thirty years. He teaches courses in the short story, James Joyce, the Black Mountain writers, the Beats, and the Literature of Addiction. His class enrollments are always largest when he teaches Charles Bukowski's novels and Edward Burns' screenplays.

Dr. Meanor has edited or co-edited five volumes of the *Dictionary of Literary Biography Series: American Short Story Writers Since WWII* (Gale Press). He has written two books: *John Cheever Revisited* (1995: Twayne-Macmillan) and *Bruce Chatwin* (1997: Twayne-Simon & Schuster). He is presently writing a book on British satirist, Will Self.

Dr. Meanor has published 200 reviews, essays, and articles. He wrote these after he stopped having hangovers in 1977. Before that, he thought a lot about writing.

Without the encouragement of Dr. Edward Kelly—who wrote much of Chapter 2—Patrick maintains he could not have completed this book.